Beautiful Purpose

Copyright © 2016 by Shayla Nicole

ISBN-13:
978-0692665961 (Shayla Nicole Publishing)

ISBN-10:
069266596X

Printed in the United States of America

First Printing, 2016

www.imshaylanicole.com

For public relation inquiries please contact
pr@imshaylanicole.com

Acknowledgements

I would like to thank everyone who encouraged me since day one. This entire concept was just an idea in my head years ago. My journey has not been an easy one and I thank everyone for their support, encouragement and contributions.

To my mother and best friend who have always been the wind beneath my wings, my support system and my life line; my manager lol. I love you and I'm glad that God designed you just for me. Thanks for the blueprint of what a phenomenal woman is like.

My two older Brothers Devin and Troy who have always been there to guide me, support me and love me. Thanks for all of your love and protection. I know you both will always stand by my side.

My best friend, and sister Sada. Thank you for being my back bone and kick-starting my mind when I ran out of ideas or needed support or simply an opinion. Thanks for taking the time and being the first one to read my book. From the designs and your research and thank you for sharing my passion! I love you Lilo!

To My father –Thank you for all of your help and support. I love you.

Uncle Allen, thank you for the encouragement and the contributions you've given me. Not just for my book. But for my everyday life.

Aunt Mari/Aunt Mommy thanks for all of your support and playing a big role in the woman I am today.

Grandma Marie - Thanks for being the root of my creativity. You always find ways of making me laugh and smile. Love you so much!

Jo-na – Thanks for helping me market my book and all of your great ideas! Forever your "boonky" :)

Aaron (my Ashford) Thanks for listening to my crazy ideas at 2 o'clock in the morning. I appreciate all of your support and advice.

Niyah- Thank You so much! For everything you have done for me! You're not only my photographer but my consultant! Thanks for your opinion and all of the effort you put into my project.

Chia- Thanks for your support and your beautiful song you made me! You're going to be a star. I know it!

To My Step Dad Ed- Thanks for your support all of your help and being proud of me.

Jarell (Jerry) I thought I was good but you thought I was great. You always saw better for me even when I didn't see it for myself. Thanks for being there from the beginning of my thinking phases. Thanks for a great friend.

Younger siblings -Kvon, Kevin, Keith, Kaliv, Kyla. I love you keep following your dreams.

Nephew and Nieces – Troy, Makiyah, Sue, Sky and Tori love you

To my friends family and supporters : Cat,Indya, Robyn, Keyona, Devon, Brian, Brandon, Pierre, Desmond, Megan, Myron, Farj, Jason, Lashae, Jordan, Kenneth, Terri, Mike, Paula, Atavia, Amanda, Quinton, Elton, Harry, Sabrika, Lavar , Kiawah, Tenia, Sean, Danielle, Jaleesa, Erika, Renee, Phene,Tia And William House, Kierra, Sheila, Joseph , Ashley, Akeem, Asha, My DaVita family and many more. If I missed your name please do not take it personally. Charge it to my memory and not my heart. God Bless!

In loving memory of Jonathan Hunt

Table of Contents

Chapter 1 🖤

"Happy Birthdaaaaaay Zuri!"

My parents entered my room a little before my alarm went off. "Ugh," I groaned, wiping my eyes. "It's not time for me to get up yet!"

"I know, sweetie, but you know we will be out of town for three days for your father's trip," my mother replied.

"But it's only 5:30, I have 15 more minutes."

"I fixed your favorite breakfasssst," my mother said in a sing-song voice.

"Oh goody," I said sarcastically, dragging myself out of bed. I hated waking up in the morning, I was a night owl. I could never go to sleep at night and in the morning I could never wake up. I dragged myself into the bathroom to do my morning routine.

I went downstairs, sat at the table, and waited for my mom to put food on my plate. We had strawberries, bananas, French toast, eggs, and turkey bacon, my favorite.

"So how does it feel to be 13?" my little brother Anthony asked.

"The same as 12."

"Well your face sure has aged," Anthony teased.

"Shut up! Gosh, you get on my nerves," I said, rolling my eyes.

"Anthony, put your iPad away," ordered mom.

"But mom, I was testing out the new software I created last night," he pleaded.

"I don't care, put it away, not at the table."

He sighed.

"What 9-year-old creates software anyway?" I said to him. "Only dweebs."

"Says the girl who always comes crying to me when her laptop isn't working right," Anthony said. I stuck my tongue out at him.

"Hello, Hello, Hellooooo!" my grandmother said as she entered the house.

My grandmother always seemed as if she was glowing, always happy.

"Today is somebody's birthdayyyy."

"Hey, granny," I said to her as we hugged.

"Hi, my teenager"

"Hey, baby," she said to Anthony, as she gave him a kiss on the forehead.

"Here, Z. I have something for you." She pulled a pretty leather box out of her purse. I opened the box – it was a beautiful necklace. It looked like a heart with copper surrounding it.

"It's beautiful, I love it!" I said with a mixture of excitement and admiration. "Thanks grandma!"

As I grabbed the necklace with my fingers to get a closer look, I felt a sharp pinch in my finger. "Ouch!" I shouted, dropping the necklace. "What is this thing made of?" I asked, looking at my finger, which was bleeding.

"Oh Zuri, you are so clumsy, just like your father," my grandmother laughed.

I examined the necklace carefully to see what had caused it to cut me but I didn't see anything that looked harmful. All I could see was some of the blood from my finger had gotten into the crevices of my necklace. I put the necklace back in the box and got up from the table to wash my hands.

"You alright, dear?" my mom asked as she rubbed my back.

"Yes, I'm fine," I said, thoroughly washing my hands. "It's just a minor cut."

I went back to the necklace to rinse it off but there was no blood on it. My grandmother must have wiped it off for me.

I finished my breakfast with my family. My mom cleared the table and my dad walked over to me, grabbed the box, and held up the necklace.

"May I?" he asked, gesturing to place it on my neck.

"Sure, as long as it doesn't poke me to death," I said hesitantly. I lifted my hair and my dad placed the necklace on my neck and gave me a kiss on my forehead.

"Happy Birthday, sweetie," he said.

"Thanks dad."

"That's a very special necklace Zuri," my grandmother stated. "Take good care of it."

"I will granny," I said as I hugged her.

I got up from the table, grabbed my backpack, and waited for my mom in the car.

"Thanks for staying with the kids, mom," dad said to granny as he gave her a hug. "It's that time of year where my job makes us all travel to Orlando for our annual team meeting" he says.

"No problem, they're angels."

"You know Zuri will have a friend with her this weekend, right? So you'll have three kids?"

"The more the merrier," she teased.

"Thanks mother," my mom said as she gave her a hug. "See ya later." Mom got in the car with Anthony and I, and drove us to our schools.

As I entered my fourth-period African American Studies class, there was a strange lady talking with our teacher Ms. Campbell. She had very dark skin, long thick hair accompanied by a headdress, along with traditional African clothing. Beside the two ladies was a table full of props. All of our desks had been cleared from the center of the room and lined along the walls. As the class entered curiously, the strange lady took her place behind her prop table and watched us go to our seats, smiling from ear to ear.

"Hello class, this is Ms. Zuba," Ms. Campbell said. "She will be joining us today. Would you like to introduce yourself, Ms. Zuba?"

"Why, hello class, or might I say *mwanafunzi*, which means student in Swahili. My name is Ms. Anya Zuba and I am from Demwii, Africa. Swahili is our main language and you will be learning some of that today. I will also tell you what tribe you belong to based upon your facial structure and family history. I have some food for you to try, some artifacts to show you, and a mini-video clip along with a dance. Sounds fun, huh?!"

"Now!" Ms. Zuba claps, "before we get to the fun part, let me tell you a little about me. I think it's only fair since I will be asking about each of you. Not because I'm nosey," she laughed at herself. "I just need to know a little about you and your family history to determine your tribe. But about me... Where do I begin?

"I was born and raised in Demwii. I have five sisters. I moved here to D.C. two years ago with my husband and son. I started teaching as a substitute for social studies but found it much more rewarding to travel to different schools, encouraging and reminding young students like you of their history. I am from the Damata tribe. People from the Damata tribe usually have high cheekbones, narrow faces, and rounded noses. We are very ambitious. And very persistent in anything that we set out to do."

"Does anyone have any questions for me?" No one raised their hands.

"You have a quiet bunch here, Ms. Campbell," Ms. Zuba stated. "I know how to take care of that," she said.

She opened a box on her table.

"I have something for you to try. This is called wagloo. It's made of wheat and berries from our Demwii wagloo sugar."

She gave everyone a piece, and some liked it, some didn't. We watched a mini-video, which was a documentary about life in Demwii. She also taught us a dance and explained some artifacts.

Next it was time for her to determine our tribe. We remained in our groups until we were called by Ms. Zuba. She finally got to me.

"My name is Zuri," I said to her.

"Zuri!" Her eyes widened.

"Did you know your name means 'beautiful' in Swahili?" we both said in unison.

"Tell me a little about yourself, when is your birthday?" Ms. Zuba asked.

"It's today actually," I laughed. "March 13."

"Why, happy birthday!" she said. "How old are you?"

"I'm 13."

"Oh wow. Tell me about your family," she said next.

"My mom was born and raised in New York, she's the only child. She went to NYU and studied Human Resources. Her mom and dad still live there. And my dad went to NYU for school as well, and studied geography. He met my mom and they got married. My grandmother is from Utabica, Africa, and I don't know much about my grandfather," I explained.

"That's interesting, I used to live north of Utabica," Ms. Zuba added. "A lot of people moved from Utabica to Demwii because of the great beast."

"The who?" I asked.

"Your grandmother never told you the story of the great beast?" she asked me.

"No," I replied curiously.

"You should ask her, it's a great story. Let's see…," she said, staring at my face.

"Your eyes are slightly lifted, your checks are widened, you look like you are from the Zenzi tribe. They are powerful people, especially the women! A lot of women from different tribes try to marry a man from the Zenzi tribe in the hopes of having a daughter, so that their daughters can become strong and have the powers of the great beast!"

She placed her hands on my face.

"Um, excuse me," I said, pulling back, startled.

"You are a Zenzi!" she said loudly, and all of the attention was on us.

"Um, ok," I said, embarrassed now. I stood up and walked to my desk to get my backpack as the bell was about to ring. She followed me over to my desk.

"Zuri, Zuri!" she said. "I shall invite you to dinner so that you can meet my son! He's about your age," she said, grabbing my arm.

"Look, lady, if this is one of those little arranged marriages so that your grandchildren can become a part of the Zenzi tribe, I'm not interested! That stuff is old and makes no sense. You're probably making this up, anyway. You're probably not even from Africa! I'm not even from Africa, I'm from D.C.!"

I put my other strap on my backpack and yanked my arm away. Ms. Zuba looked at me with a shocked face.

"Truth hurts, lady," I said, about to head for the exit, but she grabbed my arm once more.

"Oh gosh, what now?!" I said.

"Where …Did…You…Get…That…Necklace?" she said in a broken sentence, her eyes wide, staring at my necklace.

"It was a birthday gift," I said, pulling my arm away as the bell rang, and rushing out of the door.

All I heard was "ZURII!!!!! WAIT! COME BACK!" in the distance, as I rushed out of the class and outside into my mother's car.

Chapter 2 ♥

Robyn and I were sitting in my room as we were greeted with a polite knock on the door.

"Come in," I said.

In came my grandmother. "Hey sweetie," she said, "are you girls hungry?"

"Yes," we both said.

"Ok," she said, "dinner will be ready in a few," and she left the room.

As we finished dinner, Robyn and I helped my grandmother put everything away.

"Grandma?" I asked.

"Yes, dear," she replied, smiling as always.

"I had something weird happen to me today.... This lady came into my class. She said she was from Africa and she was telling us what tribes we belong to. And apparently I belong to the Zenzi tribe. Do you know anything about that?"

My grandmother's eyes lit up.

"Yes! Zuri, you are correct, our ancestors are from the Zenzi tribe. Very powerful people," grandma said.

"Yes, that's what Ms. Zuba was telling me, and she seemed to take a big interest in my necklace. I don't know, that lady was crazy!"

"She was interested in your necklace?" my grandmother asked, putting dishes up.

"Yes, I don't know what her problem was," I said.

"What tribe did Ms. Zuba say she was from, Zuri?"

"Um, I think she said Damata?" I said, unsure.

"Damata!" my grandmother said loudly, startling me a little.

"Yes, what's the Damata tribe, what are those people like?" I asked.

"Those are people who used to live in Utabica and who practiced witchcraft with spells and voodoo. They were run out of town and they made their own tribe not too far from Utabica. I didn't know they still existed!" said grandma.

"Well, granny, she said her ancestors, but I don't think there's any witchcraft around anymore," I laughed. "But then she said something about the great beast," I said, making air parenthesis. "Do you know that story grandma? The story of the great beast?"

My grandmother dropped her glass, and there was a loud crash as it broke on the floor.

"Are you ok, granny?" I said, helping her to clean up.

"I got it, Zuri. Go wait for me in the living room with your brother. I will tell you the story of the beast," she said.

Anthony, Robyn, and I all sat waiting anxiously for grandma to come in and tell us the story. She had always been so good at storytelling. Grandma entered the living room, sat on the chair, and began to tell her story......

The town of Utabica, Africa was all in a great panic. It was the year 1670, and they were just two days away from the annual return of the GREAT BEAST. The great beast was a creature of mass destruction. Coming into town, destroying many families. Many had tried to defeat him, defending the town, only to have their very own lives taken.

"I'm going to go up there," Abdul exclaimed to his mother, "it's the only way!"

"But Abdul," she cried. "You are my only son!"

"Mother, don't worry, I have been training for years. I'm finally 18 and I can fight if I choose to. I am prepared. We will go to the beast before he comes to town, I need to protect you and grandmother," explained Abdul.

"I will NOT allow it!" his mother Kina screamed. "You are forbidden! Everyone else will have to go on without you!"

"But if I cannot fight, why would you let me train and put me in the Zenzi warrior camp?" Abdul asked his mother.

"There were other things I wanted you to take from the training – brotherhood, responsibility, loyalty, but I will not allow you to go up there with everyone else, you may not come back! Go home Abdul, and do not come out until the morning when the group returns!" she shouted.

Abdul stormed off

Kina was a single mother ten years prior. Abdul was just 8 years old, his father Nathan tried to take on the beast when he came to town. He saved many lives, only to sacrifice his own. He led the beast away from the town and never came back.

Kina paced back and forth, worried about her son. She didn't know what she would do if he went and didn't come back. This was the first year the tribe had planned to do a surprise attack on the beast before he came to town. It was also the first year that Abdul was eligible to fight.

"Maybe I'll let him go next year, or the year after, if they are not able to defeat the beast," she said to herself.

She went along the hall to Abdul's room, only to find he wasn't there.

"Abdul?"

She called his name, looking in every room, before going back to his room and finding a note on his bed…

Mom:

I'm sorry to disappoint you, I shall return by morning, but I must go so that I may keep you and grandmother safe. My father risked his life to save yours, and now I shall do the same. He would have wanted it this way. I will see you in the morning, I promise.

-Love Abdul

Kina grabbed a few things and ran to her mother's house.

"Mom, I have to go find Abdul! He has defied me and gone up to the beast cave! With the rest of the tribe!!"

"Calm down my child," Kina's mother urged her.

"But mom, I have to go find Abdul!"

Kina's mother grabbed her daughter's hand and walked her into the house.

"You put him into that group so that he would become a man. So let him make his decision, as a man."

Kina sat down and began to cry. She did not sleep the whole night. She paced back and forth until she heard chaos and screams outside. The tribe has returned.

She ran outside, shouting, "Abdul! Abdul! Abdul!!!!"

She was screaming, looking through the crowd. "Abdul!!!!"

Out of the 36 men who had gone up to the cave, only four had returned. Abdul was not one of them.

"Geo!" Kina grabbed his arm.

"Where? Where is Abdul?"

"I'm sorry Kina, Abdul did not make it," he said faintly in reply.

"WHAT DO YOU MEAN!" Kina screamed

"WHERE IS ABDUL?" She pounded on his chest until she was pulled away by the people of the town.

"Well, we were all there, cornered, and the beast hovered over us like a giant. He was pretty upset and agitated. Abdul stepped in front of us, and with his sword he jumped on top of the beast and shouted for us to go! We did not want to leave him, but he begged us to go and made us promise that if he didn't return, to tell you and grandmother he loves you and he's sorry."

"I won't take that for an answer," Kina said in a stern voice, and with that she broke free from the people and went into her mother's house.

She grabbed her backpack and Nathan's old sword, and walked off into the night. She walked until dusk without stopping, she was very angry and had nothing on her mind but to get rid of the beast. The beast had taken her husband and she was almost certain her only child too, her only son, Abdul.

She finally reached the huge cave where the beast lived. She quietly threw her backpack into the bushes and took out her knife. She crept into the cave, making sure her body was pressed against the wall, not making a sound.

As she slowly walked further and further inside, she saw Abdul's backpack lying on the ground. She gasped and dropped her sword. She fell to her knees and began to cry.

But all of sudden, a huge burst of anger and rage came over her and she picked up her sword, got back up, and walked about two more miles into the cave.

That's when she saw it. She snuck up on it, very quietly. This was the perfect opportunity to get the beast while it was vulnerable and asleep. It would never have suspected that anyone would return to its cave, let alone someone on their own.

Kina raised her sword, ready to stab the beast in its heart, but all of a sudden the beast opened its huge eyes and stared at her with a single tear.

She hesitated, and lowered her sword.

"I can't do it!" she screamed, "What's wrong with me? Kina, COME ON! He took your husband and your only son!" she tried to convince herself.

The beast's single tear fell to the ground and caused the cave to rumble, making Kina fall down. She got back up and ran to the end of the cave. Out of breath, she tried to keep her composure.

She paced back and forth. "I'm going to go back in there to finish the job," she said.

She grabbed her backpack and snuck back into the cave. She went back to the beast and saw that it was now laying on its side, looking limp and pale. She snuck up to it and got a closer look. She saw that Abdul's knife was still halfway in the beast's heart, not deep enough to kill the beast instantly, but he would eventually die.

Kina started to push the knife in deeper until she made eye contact with the beast, but something made her pull it out instead. She rushed to her backpack and got some of her first aid items. She took a towel out of her bag and pressed it against the beast heart. The beast's eyes got wider and it never stopped connecting eyes with Kina's.

She pulled more first aid items and disinfectants out of her backpack and placed it on the beast's heart. She put some homemade curing medicine on its tongue, put her things back into her backpack, and started for the exit out of the cave.

"Thank you," she heard.

She turned around in shock and saw the beast still lying there.

"No no no, this can't be! I'm going crazy!"

She ran out of the cave and then ran all the way back toward the village, collapsing to the ground a few miles further on.

Kina woke up at her mother's house with a wet towel on her head.

"What happened?" she asked her mom as she woke up.

"Well I suspect you snuck out in the middle of the night to find Abdul, but never made it too far out of town. Geo found you collapsed, about five miles from here. You were pretty dehydrated," her mom explained to her.

"How long have I been out?" Kina asked.

"About six hours," her mom replied.

Kina sounded disappointed as she began to explain. "I needed to find Abdul and I couldn't even make it to the cave."

She dragged herself out of the bed and picked up her backpack.

"I'll see you later mom," she said, heading for the door.

She was trying to clamp her bag shut when her eyes rested on her half empty first aid kit.

"Oh…. No…," she said, "it's true!"

"What's true?" her mother asked.

"This can't …be," Kina said.

"What is it, dear?" her mother asked.

"I…I…I have to sit down," Kina said next, and sat down, not believing what had happened.

"What have I done?" she said softly, just louder than a whisper. "I almost….," she muttered, shaking her head in disbelief. She buried her head in her hands.

That whole day, Kina was sort of out of it. She knew what she had to do—she had to sneak off to the cave and see if what she suspected was true.

That night, she loaded her backpack and walked into the distance. She walked until dusk and arrived at the cave once more. This time, she entered more confidently and saw that the beast was awake. He growled as he laid eyes on Kina, but still looked very weak.

"I'm not going to harm you," Kina said.

She slowly put down her backpack and showed the beast her hands. She walked slowly over to the beast.

"I'm not going to harm you," she repeated. "Let me take a look at your wound."

The beast relaxed a little, and Kina removed the bandages, only to see that the wound was completely healed.

"Oh!" she exclaimed. "It looks like you're going to be ok."

Kina sat down with her back against the cave wall, looking at the beast, until she finally spoke.

"He was 18." She paused.

"The boy who stabbed you in your heart…. I told him not to go. He didn't listen to me," she said with a tear.

"He was a brave boy, my only boy. Ten years ago, you took away my husband too." She had her head in her hands.

"I miss Abdul so much," she said as she fiddled with a stick, drawing in the dirt.

"After his father died I didn't know what to do. Didn't know how to teach him to be a man. So I put him in a training tribe. Just so that he could be around other men. I couldn't raise a man. Seems like I didn't do a good job at all. He didn't even listen to me."

"Why didn't you destroy me?" the beast said.

Kina, startled, jumped up and grabbed her sword.

"You can talk? You're a female?" she said, waving her sword frantically.

"Yes and yes," the beast said. "It's been a while; I haven't had anyone to talk to."

"What do you mean?" Kina asked, still holding her sword.

"My family, they were all destroyed right front of my eyes when I was only 4 years old. I wanted to help. But I was so small and so afraid. My mom told me to hide. I shouldn't have listened. I should have been brave like your boy."

"Is that why you want to harm us?" Kina asked.

"I don't want to harm anyone. I never meant to hurt all of those people. I'm trying to find the people who took away my family and nothing will stop me. I will never forget their faces. Every year, on the anniversary of their death, I get so angry and go

20

out to seek revenge, but every time I try to find them your people try to hurt me and I have to harm them because nothing will get in the way of me finding them."

"But beast," said Kina.

"The people who destroyed your family are long gone. You have been coming to Utabica for centuries. How old...are you?"

"I'm 400," the beast exclaimed.

"400! My people do not live that long, the people who destroyed your family have probably been gone for 300 years."

"That can't be," the beast said. "How did they vanish?"

"We grow old and we die," said Kina. "You mean to tell me you have everlasting life?" she asked the beast.

"Yes, my family has been very good to God and very good to the earth, so in return we get to live together forever unless we die an unnatural death. My family are called Adoches, we are the highest form of beast there is. Kind of like a royal family. Since my family has been gone I have been living a sad, long, lonely life. Why didn't you just kill me?" the beast asked for a second time.

"I don't know," Kina said. "Maybe when I saw Abdul's knife I felt like he was still a part of you somehow. How do you heal so quickly?" Kina asked.

"Externally I heal, but inside I am still very weak," the best replied.

"I have some food," Kina said, pulling some fish out of her bag. "What is your name?" Kina asked.

"My name is Nuru," replied the beast.

"I'm Kina."

"Kina," Nuru said. "I'm really sorry about Abdul and your husband. I will let you destroy me if it will honor your family."

"I tried," Kina laughed. "I could not."

"What will you do now, Nuru?" Kina asked. "Now that you know the people you have been seeking all this time are gone?"

"Well, once I get all of my strength, I plan on moving further into the mountains where no one will ever see me again. I will give you one of my teeth so that you may take it back to the town and announce my death, so that no one will ever look for me. But right now I do not have enough strength to make that long journey. Can you help me? Please," Nuru pleaded.

"So if I help…?" Kina asked, "You will disappear and never return to harm another family?"

"Yes, I promise," Nuru responded.

For about two months, Kina snuck back and forth to the beast's cave, taking medicine and food. Throughout this time, they became best friends. Kina learned about the powers of the beast.

"I want to thank you so much, Kina," said Nuru. "I feel I will be ready next week. I will have all of my strength and will be on my way."

"It doesn't have to be this way, Nuru," Kina said. "I can explain to the people that you are not a monster. I can explain that we can all live together in harmony."

Just then, "Kina?" They heard a voice from the end of the cave.

"Oh no, Geo!" Kina jumped.

"Watch out, Kina, the beast is behind you!" Geo charged toward the beast with his sword, but Kina screamed, "No!" and jumped in front of the beast, only to have her side cut open by Geo's sword.

"What have you done?" roared the beast at Geo. The beast was closing in on Geo but Kina shouted, "No! Let him go!"

The beast growled, and Geo ran out of the cave.

"I'm going to tell everyone what you've done, Kina!" shouted Geo as he ran out of the cave. "We shall come back and both of you will be in big trouble!"

"Are you ok, Kina?" the beast said.

"I'm just getting dizzy," said Kina.

"Shall we go after him?" said the beast.

"No," she pleaded. Just let him go."

"But they will destroy us both," said the beast. "Go on, run, far away. I will stall them here."

"No," Kina said, "I will stick with you."

"Kina, if anything shall happen to us I need you to preserve my power, my gift."

"How will I do that?" Kina asked.

"You will have to destroy me," said Nuru.

"I will not harm you!" she screamed in reply.

"Kina, if you don't, the powers of the great beast will be gone forever. I want to return back to the earth. So you must take my heart out and place it into the earth so that I may be with God and my family."

"But Nuru!"

"Kina, please!"

"Ok," said Kina.

"I have one more request," added the beast.

"What's that?" Kina said in reply.

"Once you have taken my heart, place three-quarters of it into the ground, and then eat the rest. You will heal quickly. You will die as well, the power may be too overwhelming for you," Nuru warned, "but the power of the great beast will be preserved. The next female in your bloodline will possess my powers and you will be at peace with God."

Kina did as she was told. When the tribe came up to the cave seven hours later, all they could see was the limp body of the beast inside the cave. Its heart seemed to have been ripped out.

Chapter 3 ♥

"Two more weeks until summer," Robyn said as she slammed her locker. "Are you still going to Africa with the family?"

"Yes, I am," I replied, "-it will be my first time since I was three. I don't even remember it; I just see a lot of pictures. I would rather be going to Cali with you. But not for fashion camp, I want to sit on the beach somewhere."

"It should be fun," Robyn said. You get to get out of the country for a while."

"I know, I know," I replied. We entered study hall period in the library. I always used this time to actually do my homework and catch up on some studying, while Robyn just played around reading fashion magazines and texting on her phone.

"Hmmm..., let's see, what part of Africa is your grandmother from again?"

"Utabica," I answered.

"Uuuuuutabicaaaa, ahh, here we go," Robyn said, picking up a book and bringing it to our table.

I shook my head. "Robyn, I whispered, what are you doing? Shouldn't you be doing your homework or something?"

"Z, homework is for home. I'm trying to see where you're going to be this summer without me." She cracked open the book and began to look through the pictures.

"This place looks niiiiicccce," she said. "I always thought Africa had, like, little huts and everybody wore grass skirts..."

"Robyn, no, that's not true," I laughed.

She continued to skim through the photos. "Oh, look at this drawing, Zuri, I think this is the big beast your grandmother was talking about. It really is a legend. I thought your granny just made that up, you know how imaginative she can be sometimes. Looks like the people in Utabica really do believe in that old fairy tale," she laughed.

"Is this how it looks?" she asked, showed me the photograph. "Doesn't look so frightening to me..."

"Shhhh"" someone said from another table. Robyn rolled her eyes and continued to look through the pages.

"Hahaha, check this out, Zurs, this drawing looks just like you..."

"No it does not," I said, looking at the picture. "Wait a minute though, turn back." Robyn turned back to the previous page. "We do have a kind of resemblance, don't we?" I laughed. "That's awkward."

Robyn flipped through a few more pages and then closed the book. "I'm bored," she sighed.

"That's because you are supposed to be working," I said with a smirk. "You're disturbing people. Look, someone's coming over now to tell you to quiet down."

"Hi, I'm Kenneth," he said as he extended his hand to introduce himself.

"I'm Robyn, and this is my best friend Zuri," Robyn said, shaking his hand.

"Hi," I said without looking up from my book.

"She's a bookworm nerd," Robyn teased. "Have a seat," she said as she moved her backpack and patted the seat beside her. "We were just getting some studying done."

"*We*?" I said, mocking Robyn.

"Yes. We," Robyn repeated. "So what brings you here? I've never seen you before."

"I've been around," Kenneth said, his eyes locked on Zuri.

"Ahhhh, I see what's going on here," Robyn said. "I'm about to, ummmmmm, look for one of the books on my summer reading list."

"If it doesn't have anything to do with fashion or celebrity gossip, you're not going to read it over the summer," I said to her.

"Watch this for me Zuri," she said, pointing to her purse, winking at me.

"Ok." I continued to do some of my homework.

"That's a pretty name," Kenneth said.

"Thank you," I replied.

"Where does it come from?" he asked.

"It means beautiful in Swahili," I said, not once looking up from my book.

"What a beautiful name for a beautiful girl," continued Kenneth. I ignored him.

"Do you have a middle name, if you don't mind me asking?"

"Nia."

"Does that mean?" he asked, laughing. "Girl?"

"No, it actually means 'purpose' in Swahili," I replied tersely.

"Zuri Nia, beautiful purpose," he repeated, "Wow, that's a powerful name. Do you speak Swahili?"

"No, I know my grandmother is from Utabica, and that's the native language there," I told him.

"Were your parents born there too?" he asked.

"Nope," I said.

"Where are they from?" he carried on.

"What's up with the interview?" I asked Kenneth

"Sorry," he said, "you just seem interesting. I've been in this school for three years. I've always seen you but I never knew what to say. I figured I might as well talk to you now since school is just about out, and if I make a fool out of myself, I can just go to a different high school next year," he laughed.

He cracked his notebook open and begin writing. "Um, Zuri, Robyn's coming over," he said next.

"You're going to want to look at this," said Robyn, placing a book on the table. "Here's the lady again, from the other book."

"Yea, it probably is the big beast story, it's a legend there, so she's probably in a lot of the books that focus on that town," I told her, unfazed.

"That may be true, Z – but look at her in this one, she has your necklace on," Robyn went on.

"What is it saying about it?" I asked her.

"Well, it's talking about Kina and it's saying some people from the Zenzi tribe are still trying to find her," she explained.

"But that story is from centuries ago," I said.

"Are you talking about the story of Nuru?" Kenneth joined in now.

"Yes! You know that story?" I asked.

"I'm a little familiar with it. I had to do a project in my geography class last year and came across it, found it quite interesting, actually. I think it's supposed to have taken place over 300 years ago and is based on a true story. But you know those type of stories, they always say it's a true story, just to make it seem real. What's the deal with that necklace?" he asked.

"Shhhhh will you?!" someone from another table said.

"I have no idea, let's get all of the books dealing with Utabica and the big beast," I replied.

Robyn, Kenneth and I checked out four books and headed to my house after the bell rang. I text my mom to ask if Robyn and our new friend Kenneth could come over. After I received her permission, we rushed inside and placed the books on the floor.

"We have to figure this out," I said. "It's too weird if this story is hundreds of years old. Why do I have the same necklace she does, and how ironic is it that's she's from Utabica, and that her picture resembles me?"

"Well, maybe your grandmother just likes that story and they have, you know, like replicas of the necklace, kind of like a prop for the story, you know how they do," said Robyn.

"But grandma didn't say anything about the necklace. If it was such a big part of the story, why would she leave it out?" I asked.

"Well we don't know if it's a big deal or not," Robyn said.

"I wonder why she never mentioned it, she would know. Why would she give it to me if it wasn't a big deal? Let's see if we can find answers," I said as we each opened the books and began to look through them.

When I opened my book it went to a page filled with images of lines and numbers. "I don't see anything," I said as I skimmed through more pictures.

My mother came in with Anthony. "Hey sweetie, hey Robyn! Hey, who's your friend?"

"Hi, I'm Kenneth," he said, standing up and reaching out to shake my mother's hand.

"Hi Kenneth-. I don't think I've ever seen you before?" asked my mom.

"No ma'am, I'm new here," replied Kenneth.

"I thought you said you'd been at our school for three years?" I questioned.

"I have, I'm new here to your home," he stated.

"Ok, well nice meeting you," my mom responded. "I'll fix you all some snacks."

"Hi Robyn," Anthony said. "My favorite sister," he continued as gave her a hug.

"She's not even your sister, she doesn't want a little brat as a brother," I said. He stuck his tongue out at me.

"Come on Anthony, let's get our hands washed so we can fix some snacks," my mom said as she and Anthony disappeared into the kitchen.

"Does anybody see anything out of the ordinary?" I asked the others.

"Not really, why don't we just call your grandmother and ask her to clarify some things?" asked Robyn smartly.

"That would be my first choice too, but she's halfway to Africa right now. She went ahead without us-, we are meeting her there," I replied.

"Does your dad know anything about this?" she asked.

"No, he doesn't remember too much of anything prior to his car accident as a teen. By the time he started his new life he didn't care about the silly stories grandma told," I explained.

"Why do we have all of these books anyway, it's so old-fashioned and outdated, duh! Let's surf the Web instead," suggested Robyn.

"But the Web is so unreliable," said Kenneth. "Anybody with a computer and a keyboard can put something up, with no credibility to it," he stated.

"That's a fact," I agreed.

"What is this? A *Revenge of the Nerds convention*?" Robyn snorted back.

"What is THAT?" Kenneth asked, eyes wide and pointing, as a robot came out of the kitchen holding a tray with our snacks.

"Oh, that's just Darwin," I said, shaking my head and taking the snacks. "My little brother builds these stupid things."

"Well I think that's pretty clever," Kenneth said, amazed. "He's how old?" he asked.

"Nine," I said.

"Well I think that's genius for a 9-year-old!" said Kenneth.

"I like to be called intellectually intelligent," Anthony declared as he came out of the kitchen. "And Darwin is not stupid, Zuri, and don't speak like that in front of him, he's sensitive. Come on Darwin."

As Anthony and Darwin left the room, Darwin crashed into a wall and I laughed.

"See?"

"Well he's not perfect," snapped Anthony.

"I think it's the creator's error," I said to him. He stuck his tongue out at me and picked up his robot.

"He's not perfect," he repeated.

"What do you guys have going on?" my mom asked, looking at the books spread out on the floor.

"Well grandma told us a story over the weekend and it's just weird that we saw drawings of the woman Kina, from the story grandma told; she resembled me but looked older. But the crazy thing is, she had on this same necklace that I have on. The one granny gave me," I explained.

"Well maybe your grandmother knew you liked the story, so she just got a similar looking -momentum, sweetie," said mom.

"That's what I said," Robyn joined in.

"But granny gave me the necklace before she told us the story and she started acting all weird when I asked her about the big beast. I just want to know what's going on. I feel like I'm missing something here," I continued.

"You make things so complicated Zuri," my mom said. "Don't worry, sweetie."

"Ok mom," I said.

We carried on looking through the books for nearly two hours, uncovering different myths, but rarely anything to provide more information about the necklace.

"Well I have to go home," Kenneth said. "It was nice meeting you ladies."

"Do you need a ride home?" I asked him.

"No thanks, I'll be fine," he said, "I don't live too far."

"Ok, see you later," we called as Kenneth left.

"He's a cutie," Robyn elbowed me, "and he was checking you out!"

"Not interested," I said.

"Zuri, we are total opposites but somehow we function so well," Robyn said. "Just like sisters, blood couldn't make us any closer."

"Blood!" I shouted suddenly, making Robyn jump.

"Umm, what's wrong with you? Are you a vampire or something?" Robyn asked, holding her neck.

I jumped up. "Robyn, something's going on here!" I paced back and forth, agitated.

"On my birthday, when I touched the necklace it pricked my finger, and my finger bled," I said.

"Okaaaay, so you got a little boo boo," said Robyn. "So what?"

"But when I went to go clean it off or rinse it, there was nothing there. And there was no sign of anything on the necklace that could prick my finger! How ironic is that?" I explained.

"Yea, kind of strange," agreed Robyn.

"Come on," I said, grabbing Robyn by the arm as I ran up the stairs to my room.

"No running in the house Anthony!" I hear my mom say. "But moooom that's not me!" he yelled back. "It was big-foot Zuri!"

"Snitch," I hissed as I passed him.

Robyn and I went to sit at my laptop. I began to search the Web, typing in terms including- 'Kina and the beast'…. 'Utabica,' 'Kina necklace.'

An image of my necklace appeared in the search results.

"Told you to use the Web at first, but oh nooooo," said Robyn.

I read aloud from the page on the screen. *"The Zenzi's believe that Kina is a guardian; she watches and protects the people of Utabica; this necklace symbolizes the beast heart inside of the cave. They are hoping she will return and bring peace, heal the weak, and supply hope. Zenzians wear these necklaces for good luck and to symbolize power."*

"See, what did I tell ya?" Robyn said, "It's just a prop from the story."

I took a deep breath. "Had me going for a second," I said.

"Robyn!" we heard my mother call. "Your mom's here to pick you up."

"Okay, coming," she yelled back. "Ok, see ya later," she said, hugging me. "Calm down Zuri, it will be ok. Just ask granny more about her when you see her."

"I will," I said.

I followed Robyn downstairs and greeted her mom. I went back to my room and sat again at my laptop where - I began to do more research on the story of the big beast. I came across the same markings that I had seen in the library books, but this time there were a different set of numbers.

"Come in, dad," I said when I heard a knock on my door.

"How did you know I was out there?" he asked.

"I heard you coming," I said.

"How are you, sweetie?" he said as he sat on the bed.

"I'm ok, just a little confused," I told him.

"About what, sweetie?" he added.

"Well, granny told Robyn and me a story and it's just weird to me. Do you know anything about the big beast legend?" I asked him.

"What I do know is that those legends are mostly made up. There's no way a 'big beast' could ever exist. It just gives people something to occupy time and stories to pass on," he said matter-of-factly.

"Well, look dad, while I was looking in one of the books downstairs I saw a line like this," I said as I picked up a paper and pencil and drew the line, along with the numbers.

"Now look at this," I said as I pulled up the previous page in the browsing history. "And now I see this line," I said, also drawing it with the numbers. "Do you think it means something?"

"Well, Zuri, you have always been so brilliant with research and ask a lot of questions. That's a wonderful trait to have," he said. "If I had to guess, I would say it looks like coordinates pinpointing a certain location."

"Coordinates?" I asked him.

"Yes," he answered.

"To what?" I asked.

"That, I cannot tell you. Come on, I think dinner's ready." He kissed my forehead and left the room.

Coordinates? I went to the Web and typed in the numbers. _No location found_, it came back. Anthony walked into my room. "Didn't I tell you to knock before you come in?" I asked him sharply.

"The door was wide open," Anthony said.

"Come here dweeb," I said. "I'm trying to enter these coordinates but nothing's working."

"Let me see that," he said, "scoot over."

"Oh Zuri, I should really be the oldest," he said after a moment. "First off, this is not even a legitimate website."

He went to a new page and entered the coordinates. "I knew I was the brains of this family," he said proudly. "See, you have to enter it like this," he continued as he pressed enter on the keyboard.

I couldn't believe what I was reading next: "Nuru's Cave."

Chapter 4 ♥

"Did you make it there yet?"

"Yep."

"How is it?"

"Hot!!"

"Are there, like, wild zebras running around?"

"Lol! You are so crazy. No Robyn!"

"Y'all have Wi-Fi there, that's cool."

"Ha! Yes OMG Africa is nothing like you think. LOL TTYL."

"K b safe don't let the big beast get ya!"

I put my phone away as I got off of the 15-hour flight from D.C. to Utabica, Africa. I was quite tired. Mom, dad, Anthony, and I rushed through the airport as grandma waited outside to pick us up. I felt like everyone was watching me for some reason.

Grandma greeted us with a wide smile as we approached her car. "Hi my lovelies," she said!"

She got a mixture of hellos from us all. My dad and Anthony loaded all of our things into the trunk. I begged my mom to let me sit up front. It was so cool to ride on the opposite side of the car.

"Sooo, how was your flight?" grandma asked.

"It was so long," I replied. "I went to sleep about eight times and we still weren't here."

"Tell me about it," Anthony agreed. "And Zuri kept snoring," he said.

"Did not!" I shouted back.

Grandma drove us through the beautiful city of Utabica. Everything looked so bright and the breeze felt amazing. My hair blew wildly in the wind. I stuck my head out of the window, feeling like a wild lioness.

We passed beautiful beaches with white sand, exotic trees and brightly colored birds flying above us. I saw perfectly structured mountains in the distance. I think I actually did see a wild zebra running, and I laughed to myself. If I told Robyn that she'd say, "Told you so!"

We saw kids laughing and playing, families having picnics, tourists taking pictures, beautiful fruit trees, and tall, oddly shaped colorful glass buildings.

"I don't remember this place at all," I said to my grandmother.

"Yea, it's even more beautiful at night," she said, turning to me with a smile.

My crazy little brother took pictures with a camera he had made out of vintage camera pieces he found while thrifting. He always buys useless junk with his allowance. You would think a kid his age would buy video games or the latest sneakers, but no, not my brother. He was brilliant, though, not that I would ever admit it to him. Technology, programming, building things – those were his specialties. He was still a brat on his spare time, though.

We continued to drive for about ten more minutes before finally arriving at my grandmother's house. It was a nice size. A stunning building made of beautiful rust-colored bricks. She had a pretty pond in front of the house with all sorts of colorful fish in it – green, purple, red orange, you name it.

My grandmother lives in the United States but still owns her home here in Utabica. Her neighbor, Ms. Shalo always comes to check on the home in her absence. I remember her telling me the story of how my grandfather built the house with his bare hands.

"Come on in," she said. "I'll show you to your rooms."

We entered grandma's house, and it smelled like fresh lilies. It was squeaky clean from top to bottom. She led us up the stairs and showed each of us to our guest rooms.

"I'll let you all get settled in. I know you are probably tired from the flight. I'll go to the store and grab a few things, let me know if you all need anything. I will be right back," she said, turning to leave.

I went into my room and shut the door. I collapsed onto the bed, and it felt great to finally lay in one after hours of travel. I turned over and lay with my arms behind my head. I think this trip will be great after all. It's so beautiful here, I thought, I couldn't wait to explore and visit that huge mall I saw on the way here. I wondered what type of things they would have. I was sure they would have clothes you could not find in the U.S. Robyn would go crazy in there.

I fumbled with my necklace a little and noticed that it was a much brighter pink than ever, almost as if it had a glow to it. I couldn't wait to ask grandma about it when she got back. I got up, opened my suitcase, and found something more comfortable to change into. The sun was shining so beautifully so I went to the bay window, sat on the seat, and admired the beautiful land my grandmother owned. I wondered why she had away from here and come to D.C.I hoped she would let me keep this house when I got older. I opened the window to feel the nice breeze as the trees ruffled in the wind, and as the refreshing breeze hit my face I heard something flickering behind me.

I turned around to see a picture on the dresser mirror. I picked it up and examined it. It was my grandmother but when she was much younger. She was with a teenage boy and it looked like she was placing some type of badge on his jacket. They were both smiling from ear to ear. I think it was my dad. I turned to the back of the picture and it read, "Abdul – 1665."

I placed the picture back onto the dresser, and began to lay back on the bed. I closed my eyes but then something hit me. Abdul – 1665!!

44

But I was sure that was grandmother in that picture, how was she with Abdul?! In 1665?!

That can't be the same Abdul who tried to defeat the beast, I thought. Could it?!

I jumped up, grabbed the picture, and ran down to my parents' room. And began to knock on the door. "Dad! Dad!"

"Yes, Zuri," he answered in a very tired voice, "Come in."

"Dad, who is this in this picture?" I rushed to his bedside to show him the picture.

"It looks like me and your grandmother, why?" he said, squinting his eyes.

"But it can't be you, dad, this picture was taken in 1665," I pointed out to him.

"Ok, maybe it's not me," he said, turning over. "We'll look through pictures later, Zurs. I'm going to take a nap."

"But dad, this is so strange!"

"Mmm hmm," he said, closing his eyes.

I rushed out of the room and closed the door behind me. I felt so confused. It felt like an eternity before grandma got back, and I was there to open the door for her.

"You're awake", my grandmother said, smiling.

"I couldn't sleep," I told her.

"Why, honey, what's on your mind?" my grandmother asked, putting the bags on the table.

"This," I said, showing her the picture.

My grandmother looked at it as if she wanted to say more but she slowly paced her response.

"Oh," she replied simply.

"Granny," I said, "please tell me what's going on. Is this you in the picture?"

"Yes," she responded.

"Is this Abdul, from the great beast stories?" I went on.

My grandmother paused. "Yes," she said.

"But grandma how is that possible?" I asked I paced back and forth nervously. I paused before asking her, "Grandma, do you know Kina?"

My grandmother took a long pause. "Yes, Zuri, I know Kina... very well."

There was silence for about two minutes.

"Grandma? ... Are you – are you Kina?" I asked her, a bit scared.

My grandmother looked straight at me.

"Yes," she answered after another lengthy pause.

"But how is that possible?" I questioned. "Granny? But how?" I asked curiously. "Kina died, Kina would be 300-something years old by now, what's going on?" I asked.

"I was going to tell you, Zuri," she said. "I guess now is the best time since you've already kind of figured it out. You're so brilliant, you know that? You remind me so much of your dad," she said, grabbing my face. "Help granny put these groceries away and I'll tell you everything you need and want to know, I promise."

We put all of the groceries away. Grandma made us both a cool glass of tea and we sat in the hammock in the backyard. I was so excited and confused at the same time.

"Zuri," she began. "Do you remember the story of the big beast?"

"Yes," I said.

"I told you the version from the storybooks. I did not tell you what really happened," grandma said.

"So what really happened?" I questioned.

"The whole story was true up until the part where the town's people were after us," grandma started.

"The beast told me to put three-quarters of her heart into the ground and eat the rest. And after that, we would both die but my granddaughter would have the powers of the great beast. Well, I did not obey the beast. I put the three-quarters in the ground, but instead of eating the rest, I ate only a small portion of it. I then grabbed some copper from the cave and wrapped it around a tiny piece of the heart to preserve it," she explained.

"But why, grandma?" I asked.

"I didn't want the beast to die, Zuri. She didn't deserve it. I didn't know if it would save us both or not, but I took a risk. I didn't think back then, but if we had both died, the power of the great beast would have been gone forever. How could I have a granddaughter if I didn't have any more children?" grandma explained.

"So where is the other portion of the heart," I asked her. "Is it still preserved?"

"Well, Zuri, you have the remainder of the heart preserved by the copper around your neck," grandma said.

"Wow!!" I exclaimed, looking down at my necklace.

"Once your blood, well, your Zenzi blood touches it, you are in sync with it," grandma said.

"No wonder it pinched me on my birthday! Wait a minute, wait a minute," I said, and paused. "So, if you're alive, did the beast die?"

"No Zuri, we are all alive," grandma said.

"*We* are all? *Who* is alive?" I asked.

"Well, eating a portion of the heart gave me powers. I can live for all eternity if I choose to, among other things. I can also bring things back to life," grandma said.

"So you brought the beast back to life?" I asked.

"No, when I preserved the heart the beast's spirit was still alive. She chose to switch form to a human so that the Zenzians wouldn't try to harm her if they were to come across her. But just for safety we both left Africa and moved to D.C. Of course, she didn't like it there.......," my grandmother trailed off. "It was too cold for her, so she came back about 100 years later," she laughed. "Anyhow," she said, shaking her head. "I brought Abdul back."

My eyes widened. "My dad is Abdul!!?" I asked.

"Shhh, shh," my grandmother urged. "Yes, he is."

"So how old is my dad?" I questioned.

"It took me hundreds of years to gain enough strength to be able to do that, Zuri. It takes a lot of power to bring someone back to life. And a lot of practice. It drains a lot of energy that can take years to get back. Technically, I only brought your father back about 27 years ago," she explained.

"Does he know?" I asked.

"Honestly, I don't know," she answered. "If he does know and is trying to forget, I don't want to remind him, it could be traumatic for him. And if he doesn't know, I don't want to frighten him" she said.

"So when you brought him back he was the same age as when he died?" I asked.

"Yes," my grandmother stated. "Are you ok, Zuri?"

"Yes, grandma, I just think this is beyond awesome!" I told her. "This is a lot of information to take in!"

"So does my dad have any childhood memories?" I asked next.

"Not really," granny said.

"All he remembers is waking up out of a coma. I told him he was in a bad car accident. I plan on telling him the truth one day, but how do you tell someone that the life that they know has a deep past behind it?" my grandmother asked.

"There's more, Zuri," she continued. "Since you are my granddaughter you will unlock and possess the powers of the beast. So you have a great gift and an important job..." She was cut off as we heard another voice.

"Missy!" Ms. Shalo said as she entered the yard.

"Hey, Nuru!" grandma said.

"Hey, Kina!" they teased.

"It's been a while since we could call each other our real names around others,".... said Nuru.

"You're the beast?" I whispered.

"Yes," she whispered back. I got up and hugged her, and she smiled.

"This is so amazing, you guys are like a million years old," I said.

"Heeey," Nuru said.

We're not that old," grandma laughed.

"I heard you telling the story, Kina, so I thought I'd come over to help" said Nuru.

"You heard her telling the story?" I questioned. "You have like bionic ears or something?"

"Something like that," she said.

"Tell me about me, how I will become powerful," I asked.

"Well you are already powerful Zuri, you just don't know how to utilize it. All you have to do is properly train," grandma said.

"No biggie, when can we get started?" I asked.

"Zuri, seriously," my grandmother said in a stern voice. "This is not a joke. I know how exciting it may be for a 13-year-old, but you must be responsible and careful. And it is a big biggie.

The truth is, we need you. You are the missing link. So it is imperative that you take your training and powers seriously," she went on.

"I will," I said. "What do you guys need me for?" I asked. "What am I training for?"

"We will explain all of that later, I think you've had enough information for one day. Why don't you go lie down for a second?" my grandmother insisted. "This is a lot of information for one day. We will start with training first thing in the morning, ok?"

"Ok." I hugged them both and went into the house. I almost collapsed on the bed, either from jet lag or from too much excitement about what was to come.

"Let's hope this works," Nuru said to my grandmother outside.

"Oh it will," she said. "Zenzi's are brilliant."

Chapter 5 ♥

I woke up to see my little brother looking over me.

"She's aliiiiive!" he yelled out.

"Of course I'm alive, brat, what time is it?" I said.

"Well, it's nine o'clock," he replied.

I looked to the window and saw the sun was shining bright. "You mean nine in the morning?" I asked in disbelief.

"Duh!" he said, shaking his head.

"I slept the rest of the day until morning?" I questioned.

"Yes, morning usually comes after the night Zuri, plus I tried to wake you up for dinner last night but you wouldn't budge. I even sent Darwin in here," he told me.

"Why'd you bring that stupid thing anyway?" I asked.

"He's not stupid, Zuri, he just has a few kinks I need to work out. His programming is off," Anthony explained. I shook my head.

"Anyhow, grandma said to leave you alone, that you needed to recharge… whatever that means. Well I've done my job here, go brush your teeth, you smell like yesterday. Oh, and um, breakfast is ready downstairs. I'm out," he said as he left, putting up the peace sign. "Come on Darwin," he called out to his robot. I shook my head, my little brother thought he was so hip. The hippest nerd I've ever met.

I got up, washed my face, and brushed my teeth. I headed downstairs to see that grandma had a variety of fresh fruit and homemade Utabica specialties. I sat down and ate as my mom cleaned the breakfast dishes.

"You ready for today?" my grandmother winked at me.

"I am sooooo excited," I said. "I can't wait!"

"What are y'all doing today?" my nosey brother asked.

"We are going shopping for pretty dresses and skirts," I said to him.

"Yuck, dad and I are going to the beach to go windsurfing," he said. "Mom's probably going to just sunbathe and read her book, sounds pretty boring to me," he continued, "but then we are having a picnic on the beach. And while you were being lazy sleeping, dad and I built waterproofing mechanisms that will enhance our windsurfing experiment," he added.

"A waterproofing what?" I questioned, "Where'd you all find this kid?" I asked. "Can you be a normal 9-year-old, for once?" I asked him.

"Normal is boring, and sounds like you're going to miss all the fun, Zurs," Anthony said. "I'm going to go get my swim gear." He headed up the stairs.

"He is such a nerd," I said after he left.

"Don't be so hard on him Zuri, you know your brother loves his experiments and inventions. Encourage him, he looks up to you," my mom said, and she kissed my cheek.

"I think I have everything washed and put away," my mother said to my grandmother.

"Thanks honey, you really didn't have to," came grandma's reply.

"Well momma, it's the least I can do for you, opening up your home to us," said mom.

"Come on sweetie, you're family," replied grandma.

"You sure you guys don't want to come to the beach with us?" mom asked.

"I'm sure, sweetie," grandma said to mom, "Zuri and I will be just fine, won't we honey?" see added as she squeezed my shoulders.

"Yes, indeed," I said, smiling and eating my breakfast.

"Ooookay," mom said as she left to get dressed for the beach. As I finished my breakfast, my family came downstairs. I hugged them and waved goodbye. I was so excited to learn what was ahead for me.

"Ok, Zuri, put on your athletic wear and meet me out in the yard," grandma said as soon as they'd gone.

I went upstairs, took my shower, got dressed, and headed toward the backyard.

"Hey grandma," I said, "you look kind of cute in your athletic wear," I teased.

She looked at me sternly and just said, "Follow me."

"Okaaaay," I replied.

My grandmother zipped to the end of the yard, where the trees were, almost as fast as lightning, and waited there for me.

"Am I supposed to do that?" I yelled after her. She didn't answer. "Ummm, ok," I said to myself. I rubbed my necklace and began to run but I was going my normal speed. I thought I would be fast ... I thought wrong.

I finally made it to where granny was gasping for air. "You...sure... are... fast... for an old lady," I said, gasping for air.

"To be fast you must make everything around you slow down," came her mysterious reply. "Follow me."

"Please don't run anymore grandma, I don't think I can run any further," I pleaded with her.

Grandma took a few steps forward, then stooped down, grabbed a handful of dirt, and threw it into the air, waving her hands as if she were parting the air. The dirt stopped in midair, split into two separate parts, and then fell to the ground. I heard the ground shaking and the trees in front of us split, creating a walkway. I nervously grabbed my grandmother's hand. We walked forward as the trees began to go back into their original spot behind us. It seemed to me as if we were getting chased by trees.

Finally, we made it to the end of the walkway. There was an open field, and Nuru was standing there waiting for us. I looked behind us and there was no walkway, just a bunch of trees all together. I admit I was quite nervous.

"Hello, Zuri," Nuru said.

"Hey," I said.

"Are you ready to get started?" she asked.

"Yes," I said, as I let go of my grandmother's hand. "I'm ready."

"Let me start off by telling you what we are training for. We have an important mission Zuri, and you are our only hope," Nuru began to explain.

"Sheesh, don't put so much pressure on a sister," I laughed. Nobody laughed with me.

"Zuri," Nuru began again, "I am very thankful Kina spared my life. And I am extremely happy that we were both able to survive and live as long as we have. However, because Kina did not insert all of my heart into the earth, there is unbalance in Africa, things have not happened that were supposed to happen. Besides, I have lived long enough. I would like to be with my family, you see. If things don't balance out soon Utabica could suffer greatly. Wars may break out amongst several tribes. Different tribes are forming—the Kina supporters and the non-Kina supporters. Some think she is harmful, a witch even. Some think she is a peacemaker. You see Zuri, in order to save Utabica, I must die," Nuru said.

"But I'm not going to destroy you," I said.

"Zuri, I do not need you to destroy me. I just need you to return the last piece of my heart to the exact location where Kina buried the other portion" she said as she touched my necklace. "Though my body will vanish, my spirit will remain. I will be one with my family again," Nuru said. "No longer will tribes look for me or Kina, and Utabica will be peaceful again."

"Ok, so you need me to put this necklace into the ground? That sounds easy," I said.

"Oh, but it is not," my grandmother said. "First we need to pinpoint the area of Nuru's cave... you see it has been hundreds of years, and since then it may have collapsed. You have to find the exact location of the cave, then you must place the final piece inside. When you're close you will know because your necklace will turn a bright pink."

"It did that yesterday," I said. "I had never seen it before."

"Probably because technically you are closer to it than before," grandma said.

"You are in Utabica now, not D.C. I know I wrote the coordinates somewhere, I think they're in an old book but I have no clue where. I wrote them down because people of the Damata tribe were hot on my trail. I tried to go back to the location to place the final piece of it in the earth a week after I buried the first portion, but the Damata tribe stood guard constantly in case the beast would return. I needed to write it down somewhere I wouldn't forget, and as soon as I got a chance I wrote it in a school textbook your father had, but, oh, it had to be a hundred years or so back," she continued.

"School textbook?" I asked. "Well I remember my dad donating books to my school library. When Robyn, Kenneth and I were researching Utabica, I saw numbers written in a book. My dad said they were coordinates, so Anthony help me decode the numbers online. When we searched 65° 32' 15" the result was Nuru."

"Oh Zuri! You are so smart, that sounds right! You know the coordinates; we are one step closer." Nuru and Kina jumped with glee.

"OK, so let's go put the necklace into the ground now that we know where to go," I said.

"Well, Zuri, in order to put the necklace in the ground you have to go back in time to the exact spot." said Nuru.

"Back in time," I thought to myself. What had I gotten myself into? Was this a dream? My vision clouded as I listened to Nuru explain just how it would be possible for me to travel through time. She said we must open a portal.

"So I'm just going to Utabica back into the 1600s, finding the cave, and placing the rest of the heart into the earth? Once I do that I can just come back and everything will be ok? Will I still have my powers?" I asked.

"Yes Zuri, you will always have your powers," said Nuru.

"Yes!" I said, pleased. "Wait a minute, though, will I live to be, like, 300 years old, too?"

"Only if you chose to Zuri," said Grandma.

"Then who will get the powers after me?" I asked.

"Your granddaughter," said Nuru.

"What if I don't have children, or what if my children don't have children, or what if my children's children are all boys?"

My grandmother laughed. "Then the next girl in the family line will get the powers."

"So if Anthony has a daughter, she will have them?" I asked, trying to make sense of it all.

"Yes Zuri," answered Nuru.

"Only you can place the necklace in the earth Zuri" grandma continued. "Do not let anyone else put your necklace into the ground. If the wrong hands get ahold of it, everything that you know now will change."

"You see, if anyone besides our bloodline places it in the ground, it will upset the earth, the ground may cave in, and everything may go terribly wrong. You see... everything needs to go as planned, we are counting on you, Zuri. We know you can do it, you are the Zenzi granddaughter of Kina, beast blood runs in your veins. You have great power!" grandma said, her voicing getting more excited.

"You guys sure I can do this? I mean, this is a lot of pressure," I asked.

"I'm positive," my grandmother said.

"I mean, you guys will be there, right? To guide me, coach me?" I asked.

"We can't, Zuri. We cannot coexist with our past. You weren't born during that time and didn't exist. That's why we must train you. You have to know how to use your powers in case you have to defend yourself," explained Nuru,

"DEFEND myself! From who?" I asked, getting nervous now.

"Well, Zuri, if you go into town, you do know you will be back at the same moment when Geo and the rest of the tribe were looking for Kina. In case you run into them you may need to defend yourself. Don't worry Zuri, we will not send you on your way without the right skills and equipment, so just trust us," said grandma.

"I trust you," I said sternly. Just at that moment I had never felt so much responsibility in my entire life. I knew I had an important mission, I had a "purpose."

"I'm ready," I said.

Chapter 6 ♥

As we stood in the field my grandmother spoke softly but sternly. "First thing you have to do, Zuri, is relax, close your eyes. Erase everything negative from your mind, jussssst relax, close your eyes, become one with the earth. Inhale.... exhale ... The earth is your family ... You love the earth and the earth loves you." Nuru had her eyes closed, and so did Kina. I looked around, thinking 'this is insane.' I felt like I wanted to laugh.

"Inhale. Exhale," she repeated. "Feel the wind from the tips of your fingers to the tips of your hair. Become one. You take care of the earth, the earth will take care of you. Inhale. Exhale. Can you feel it, Zuri?" Nuru asked, her eyes closed. "Can you feel it?"

"Ummm, I can't feel anything," I said.

"You have not relaxed," my grandmother stated. "Think of nothing, Zuri. Nothing."

"But isn't thinking of nothing still thinking of something?" I asked.

"Relax, Zuri, relax… relax relaaaaax, breathe, relax, clear your head, clear your thoughts relax….relax….. Re------."

All of a sudden Nuru's voice had faded out. All I could hear was the sound of wings flapping, trees moving. I could hear and smell the air. I could smell fresh flowers and felt the sun on my skin. I felt as if I was floating and could feel the grass swaying under my feet, I heard water running from afar. I opened my eyes to see my grandmother and Nuru looking at me.

"That was awesome!" I said.

"Well Zuri, you need to be in touch with the earth every second of the day. It may be hard to turn on and off now, but with practice and when you are truly one it will never go away. You will be able to control everything dealing with nature," explained Nuru.

"This is so cool," I said, still in amazement. "Is there like some sort of spell or something I have to say, I mean, what exactly can I do?"

"Once you are one with the earth, all you have to do is think it in your mind. It will listen to you. Your mind and your heart are the most powerful things, Zuri. That's why it is important to clear everything negative. Use your hands for balance and use your mind to lead everything in the direction that you need it to go. Follow your heart, both the one in your chest and the one you are wearing. Trust nature, trust your senses. Now I want you to go back to the same place you were just in, Zuri. Try doing it with your eyes open this time. And then I want you to run. Run to the end of the field and come back," Nuru said.

I looked at her strangely. "You telling me you want me to run to the end of the field? But I don't see where it ends," I said. "Can we try the next thing?" I said. "I'm not ready!"

"Zuri," my grandmother said. "You can do it. It's very simple you see. Just relax, just like you did before. Become one with the earth. Relax, you can slow everything down. So that you may move. Swiftly. Become the wind Zuri."

I tried to zone out with my eyes open, but there were too many distractions. I began to run but it was my normal pace. I started to get very frustrated with myself.

"Zuri, you have to believe you can do it. You're telling yourself that you can do it but you don't believe it," shouted grandma.

"1-2-3," I counted. I zoned out once more and began to run, but it was still at my normal pace. "Why isn't it working?" I groaned.

"It's not going to come easy, Zuri," Nuru said. "You have to really, really focus. Trust yourself, believe it, feel it."

I closed my eyes and zoned out, went back to the same place that I was when I could feel the nature. I slowly opened my eyes. My vision was very clear and bright, everything looked beautiful and more in color than I remember the earth being. I began to run, I felt as if I were moving in slow motion, only to stop at a lake. I must have made it to the end.

I didn't feel tired or anything, I wondered how long it had taken me to get here. I heard the birds singing and a deer getting a drink from the lake. I walked over to the lake to see beautiful tropical fish. I slowly placed my hand in the water and a fish came up to it, making me pull it back.

"Since when do fish swim up to your hand?"

I could hear Nuru speaking. "You think she's alright?"

"I'm sure she's fine," my grandmother said. "She'll be ok."

"Maybe I should go look for her, surely she would have made it there by now? But it's at least seven miles to the end," I heard Nuru continue.

"Seven miles!" I gasped, I got here in seconds. And how the heck could I hear them seven miles away? I decided to head back to them. I grabbed a pretty flower from one of the trees and stuck it in my hair. I made sure I was focused and zoned out, and I ran in what seemed like slow motion, but it was actually lightning speed, back to my grandmother and Nuru.

Nuru smiled. "Hey," she said with a sigh of relief. "I'm glad you made it."

"Yea, I could hear you were worried, so I decided to come back sooner," I giggled.

"You heard?" my grandmother asked.

"Yea," I said. "You told Nuru not to worry and that I would be ok." They both looked at each other, confused.

"How far did you get?" asked Nuru.

"I went to the lake, that was the end right?" I asked.

"Yes Zuri, you can hear that far away?" asked Nuru.

"Um, yea," I said, "That's a part of my powers, right?"

"Well I can't hear that far," said my grandmother. "I can only hear about a mile away. That's amazing," she said. "Wonder what other powers you have that are stronger than mine."

"Wish I could fly," I laughed. I started flapping my arms and nothing happened. "It was worth a try," I laughed. "What's next?"

"We have to build your strength," Nuru said.

Nuru walked over to a tree and lightly pushed it. It fell down. "Pick it up," she said to me.

"That tree?" I said, pointing to it.

"Yup," she said. "That tree."

"What about if we start off with something light, like that one," I said, and pointed to a much smaller, skinnier tree.

"Zuri," my grandma said with seriousness.

"Ok, ok." I stretched a little and then attempted to pick it up... Nothing. "What's the secret to this?" I asked, sweating a little as I try to pick the huge tree up. "Whew," I said, and sat down on it.

"First off, lift from your knees. And have you forgotten already Zuri?" my grandmother said. "Your mind and heart are the most powerful things. Just believe that you have the strength."

I got up and tried again to lift the tree; I couldn't. By this time, I was really frustrated.

"Relax. Take your time," Nuru insisted.

Once again, I went to the tree and began to lift it. Again I struggled.

"Use your knees," my grandmother said. "And believe that you can lift the tree. You are the tree; you are the air!"

67

I continued to lift the tree. It began to lift a little, and then it dropped right on my foot!

"AAAAH!" I cried, "This is so stupid, I don't know why I have to lift this stupid tree anyway! I'm going home!" I cried. "I don't want to do this anymore. My foot is broken, I know it!" I said, as I screamed and began limping towards the house.

"Zuri?" my grandmother said.

"I quit, grandma," I said as I continued to limp. "I don't know what sense it makes to make a 13-year-old girl lift a 300-pound tree," I complained. "That's impossible for me to do. This is so crazy," I screamed.

"Zuri?" grandma called again.

"I'm done," I said. "I have to call an ambulance."

"Zuri Nia!" my grandmother yelled. I stopped in my tracks and turned toward her. "Just stop it Zuri," my grandmother said. Nuru was snickering.

"What's so funny?" I asked, sort of upset. I didn't think me being injured was any type of joke. I was in pain!

"Zuri, nothing is wrong with your foot," said grandma.

"What do you mean?" I said. "I just dropped a 300-pound tree on my foot!"

"Actually its 500 pounds, and you're ok. Just walk normally Zuri."

"Huh?" I said, confused.

"Zuri," Nuru said. "If a 500-pound tree fell on someone's foot, that foot would in fact be broken, they probably wouldn't even be able to walk on it, not even limp. And they would probably still be crying," she laughed. "You, on the other hand, no doubt it hurts, but let's see in about 5...4...3...2 and...uhhhhhh, 1! Your foot should be back to normal. Just walk."

I looked at my foot and wiggled it a bit. I put it on the ground and slowly and carefully took a few steps. It was normal!

"Oh...," I smiled. "I knew that!" I said, trying not to sound surprised.

My grandmother shook her head. "Stop saying you can't do things, Zuri, there is power in your tongue. Say and believe that you can conquer anything! We've had enough for one day, let's get back to the house. It's your turn to open the pathway," said grandma.

"Now, in order to split the trees, Zuri, you must take the dirt," she continued. "Throw it in the air and use your hands to allow the dirt to fall back into place. This is your promise to the earth that even though you have moved the trees temporarily, you will put them back in their place. Now, let's try it."

I grabbed a handful of dirt and threw it in the air, but before I could part it, it fell to the ground. "Hmm..." I tried once more, and it did the same thing. "What am I doing wrong?" I said. "Why won't it stay?"

You did not tell it to stay Zuri," my grandmother said. "Slow it down, think with your mind, Zuri. Pause everything."

I lifted the dirt once more. It stayed still, then I parted it in the air and thought for the trees to part. The ground rumbled and the trees parted. I could see grandma's house in the distance. "I'll race y'all," I said to granny and Nuru.

I zoned out and began to run in a dash. I saw a flash in front of me and shortly after, another flash. I finally reached the house and looked back to the trees, the last of them were closing the pathway returning to their original positions.

"What took you so long?" I heard from behind me. Granny and Nuru were sitting on the patio furniture. "But---!" I looked into the woods. "How did y'all do that?" I laughed. "So I guess the two flashes I saw were you two?" We all laughed. "I've been outrun by 400-year-olds!"

"Hey! I beg your pardon, young lady, I'm only about 345," my granny said.

"Thanks for the training," I said to each of them. "Same time tomorrow?"

"That will work," Nuru said.

"K," I replied, and went inside to take a shower while Nuru helped granny fix dinner.

Chapter 7 🖤

"So you're like superwoman mixed with nature girl?" asked Robyn as she FaceTimed me.

"I guess you could say that," I laughed.

"You have to plant that necklace by yourself, that's pretty scary, more power to you Zurs," she said.

"Actually, it's not scary at all," I said. "I'm excited, I can hardly wait."

"This all seems like a movie or something," Robyn laughed.

"This Africa trip is more exciting than I expected," I said as I propped my iPad on my pillow.

"My best friend is a superhero," she said

"Shhhh!" I told her.

"Can I be your sidekick? Zuri and Robyn! Wait, Robyn is already taken as a sidekick name...." She pouted as she thought about this. "Well I'll think of something." We both laughed.

"So how's fashion camp going for you?" I asked

"I love it!" she exclaimed. "It's really cool, I've learned so many useful tips. And every three days we get a theme and we have to create a look for it. We get to go shopping for fabrics and I have, like, a whole kit! Its sooo fun, I love Cali too, the weather here is great. How's the weather there?"

"Oh it's beautiful," I said. "Much better than home."

"Well, got to go help my roommate with her outfit, talk to ya later sis, love ya," Robyn said.

"Love you too, Robyn," I replied.

I went downstairs and had dinner with my family. As we were eating I looked at my dad smiling and laughing, playing with Anthony. I realized how precious life was. I looked at granny, who was a strong, powerful woman who never gave up on bringing life to her son. I mean, it took her hundreds of years to bring my dad back and she never gave up. That thought alone made me determined to complete this task and do whatever I had to do. As I watched Nuru and my mom talking I came up with a new appreciation for Nuru and how far trust and friendship goes. She trusted my grandmother with her gift. And I'm so thankful for it.

"Zuri!" my little brother Anthony said. "You were daydreaming; mom was talking to you."

"Oh," I said. "Yes mom?"

"You're awfully quiet and you haven't eaten anything yet," mom said. I just smiled, and began to eat my food. After dinner was done, Anthony and I cleaned up the dishes.

"Did you have fun at the beach?" I asked him.

"Yea, it was pretty cool," he said. "Oh yea, I forgot to tell you. I saw your friend there."

"Who?" I said.

"Ummmm, the dude who came over our house?"

I thought for a second. "Kenneth?"

"Yea, that's his name," said Anthony.

"That's impossible," I said.

"I'm sure it was him", Anthony replied.

"That's odd if it was." I said. "Well did you say something to him?"

"He didn't see me, he looked like he was lost or something," said Anthony.

"Was he with anybody?" I asked.

"No, he was by himself."

"Are you sure, Anthony? You sure it was Kenneth?" I pressed him.

"Yea, I remember him," he said as he dried the dishes.

It seemed a little odd that Kenneth would be here in Utabica. If he knew he was coming, why didn't he tell me? He knew I was coming here. I decided I would try to contact him later. I shook that thought off and put away my last dish. I went to my room and sat on the bed. I was very tired, but excited too. I picked up my iPad and tried to connect to Kenneth. After what seemed like forever, he answered.

"Kenneth!" I began

"Hey, Zuri," he said.

"I haven't heard from you in a while," I replied. "I have so much to tell you. How are you?"

"I'm doing fine," he said.

"Where are you?" I asked.

"Huh?" he said.

"Where are you?" I repeated. He seemed a little hesitant.

"Well, my mom sent me here to Africa this summer to be with my dad. I really didn't want to come," he replied.

"I thought your dad was in D.C., too?" I asked.

"He's in the military," Kenneth answered.

"Well that's awesome Kenneth! Why didn't you tell me you were coming?" I asked.

"The news was kind of sprung right on me unexpectedly," he sighed.

"Don't seem so down about it, it's really not that bad. Maybe we can hang out. How far are you from Utabica?" I asked him.

"Errrr, probably about 20 minutes I think?" he answered.

"My brother said he saw you at the beach today." I told him.

"Yea I was there. It was kind of cool," he said. "Until I lost my cellphone. I don't know why I took it to the beach anyway. I just got here yesterday," he continued. "It was a very long trip. All I wanted to do when I got here was sleep. Have you heard from Robyn?" he asked.

"Yea, she's doing great in fashion school. She's really enjoying it. Hey, maybe you can help me!" I said

"Help you? Help you with what?" he asked.

"I have something very important I must do," I said.

"Like what?" he asked.

"It's top secret, Kenneth. You can't tell anyone," I warned him.

"Tell anyone what?"

"I want to tell you in person," I said. "Can you meet me at the beach?"

"Yea, sure, is everything ok, Zuri?" he asked, sounding concerned.

"Yea, everything is fine, meet me in 30 minutes," I told him.

I gathered a bunch of my things, put them in my backpack, and readied myself. Maybe I wouldn't have to do this whole journey alone, after all.

"I'll be back," I said as I walked past my parents and grandmother in the living room.

"Where are you going?" my mom asked.

"Just to take a walk," I said.

"Take your brother with you," mom called after me.

"But mom, I'll be ok. I'm just going down the street," I told her.

"I don't care, Zuri, I don't want you going anywhere alone. You're not familiar with the area," she added.

"I think she will be fine," my grandmother butted in.

"Here Zuri, take my cell," grandma said, handing me her cellphone. "If you need anything just call or we will be in touch with you." She winked at me. "Is that ok dear?" she asked my mother.

"It's fine," said mom. "Be safe Zuri."

"I will," I said.

I walked away from the house to get out of sight, made sure no one was watching, and then dashed to the beach. When I got to the beach Kenneth was not there yet. I wondered how long it would take him to get there. While waiting, I took my shoes off and walked along the shore. Planting my toes in the sand I wondered if I could swim or breathe underwater. I laughed at that thought.

I saw Kenneth in the distance, so I walked up behind him and placed my hands over his eyes.

"Um, who could this be? Maybe the only person I know here. Zuri?" he said sarcastically.

"Hey, Kenneth," I said.

He laughed. "Hey, what's up?" he asked.

"I have soooo much to tell you," I said, excited. "I have an important mission to go on, and I need your help. You know the big beast story right?"

"Vaguely, but yea," he said.

"Well, my grandmother is Kina," I whispered to him.

"That's impossible," he said. "That doesn't make sense."

"But it does, Kenneth. You see, I'm the daughter of Abdul. Kina brought him back. And now it's my responsibility to put my necklace into the earth so that everything balances out!" I said.

"I'm soooooo lost," he said, "but count me in. Anything is better than sitting on the base all day. Where is it?"

"Well we kind of have to go back in time."

Kenneth laughed. "You have got to be kidding me, is this some sort of joke, Zuri?"

"I know how strange this may sound Kenneth," I chuckled a little. "But no! This is not a joke."

He looked at me. "Well, ok! Let's go," he said.

"I have a feeling you don't believe me," I said.

"It does sound a little fairy-taleish, but I'm down!" he replied. "I would rather be playing adventure time with you than be stuck with my dad. All he wants to do is convince me to join ROTC in high school and to join the military. And if he tells me another story I'm going to fall asleep he laughed. "I feel like he doesn't pay me any attention or encourage me to do anything that I want to do. When I talk to him he never really listens." Kenneth looked down. "So when's the big day?" he asked, trying to lighten the mood.

"Probably within the next two days," I said.

"Cool," he shrugged.

We spent about 30 minutes talking and laughing and planning our tactics. We played the what-if game and imagined what it would be like to travel in time.

It was getting a little late, so we decided to go back home.

"Will you be ok getting home?" he asked. "Do you need me to walk you there?"

"No, I'll be fine," I said.

"No Zuri, I'll walk you home, maybe your grandmother can take me back to base," he insisted.

"Kenneth, no, really, it's fine," I assured him.

"Zuri," he paused.

"Kenneth, I'm fine," I said again.

"Well call me as soon as you get in," he said. "Promise?"

"I promise," I said. He hugged me and said goodbye.

I walked off toward granny's, and when Kenneth was out of sight I dashed back to her house. I walked into the house and placed my backpack on the floor.

"What's with the goofy grin?" Anthony said as I came in, startling me a little.

"You are such a creep Anthony," I said. I grabbed my backpack and went into my room. I waited about five minutes, then FaceTimed Kenneth.

"I'm home," I said.

"You must not be very far from the beach," he said.

"Nope, not at all. Ok, I'll probably see you tomorrow," I said. "Goodnight."

"Night, Zuri."

Chapter 8 ♥

I met grandma and Nuru out in the open field.

"What are we practicing today?" I asked.

"Well Zuri, we need to work on your combat and your...," Grandma threw a ball at me, and I caught it, "...reflexes," she continued. "Not bad," she commended me.

"Combat? Combat for what?" I asked.

"Well Zuri, it's just in case. We are not sure you will have to use these skills, but, worst case scenario, someone may try to stop you from entering Nuru's cave. I just want to make sure that you are prepared," grandma continued.

"Well I'll have some help," I said.

"What do you mean?" she asked.

"My friend Kenneth, from D.C. He's here and he's agreed to go with me," I told them.

"You told someone else?" Nuru asked me.

"Was I not supposed to?" I asked, feeling guilty.

"Don't tell anyone else, ok Zuri," Nuru said. "No one. He cannot go with you, it's too dangerous."

"I'll protect him; I'll protect us both. Imagine being a teenager going someplace far in time, all alone. It's kind of scary," I said. "At least I'll have someone there with me."

"It's too risky, Zuri, what if you can't protect him? What do we tell his parents if their son doesn't come back?" asked Grandma.

"What do you tell mine if I don't come back?" I asked. There was a moment of silence.

"You will," my grandmother said. "There's no question about that one. But we cannot allow him to go. You don't need any distractions."

"Distractions from what?" I asked. "If anything he would be an asset. Another set of eyes and ears. He could help me. It's better to travel in pairs," I said. "Please. I know that I am capable of doing this alone but I need a friend. It's already a lot for me to take on alone. Now that he already knows what's going on, what could be so bad about it?"

Nuru walked away from us.

"Zuri," my grandmother said. "I understand. You are so bright and responsible, sometimes I forget that you are just a kid. I'll talk with Nuru. Maybe it would be a good idea to have someone go with you."

"Thanks granny," I said, and gave her a hug. "Now let's get to work."

I practiced running laps to the pond and back, increasing my speed each time. I lifted the tree this time without that much of a struggle. I learned to punch, jab, duck, I even practiced gymnastics. This seemed to go on for hours. Somehow I was not tired.

"Well, good job Zuri," Nuru said. "You catch on really fast. Do you think you're ready?"

"I'm ready to leave now," I joked. "How long will it take me?" I asked.

"Well, in real time, about a day, two days in the past are equivalent to one day now," explained grandma. "Don't worry, I'll tell your mom we are together. Do you have any questions?"

"How do I get back home?" I asked.

"Just reopen the portal. But once you set foot back on this side Zuri, you cannot go back," added grandma.

"What if I don't make it to the cave, will Nuru still be able to be with her family?"

"Nuru could be with her family now if she wanted to Zuri, she's lived long enough," said grandma.

"Then what is she waiting for?" I asked, more confused now.

"Nuru wanted to make sure I was alright and make sure that I was protected. Nuru is my best friend. She wants to make sure everything here will be alright when she leaves and she believes the only way to make everything right is to make sure that her heart is in the ground like it was supposed to be," explained grandma.

"But I like this necklace," I teased.

"I'll make you another one," granny said.

"But I want this one, its real!" I protested.

"Where is this Kenneth guy? I would like to meet him," Nuru said.

"Ok, I'll give him a call," I said.

I dashed to the house and called Kenneth. About an hour later, he arrived at the house on a bicycle. "Woo," he said, sweating. "This is not as close to the beach as I thought."

I walked with him around to the backyard.

"Where's your grandmother?" he asked.

"She's around," I told him.

I grabbed dirt from ground, split it, and the trees separated.

Kenneth's eyes lit up and his jaw dropped.

"You have got to be kidding! That is super cool Zuri! How did you do that!" he rambled on.

I grabbed his arm and dashed into the woods, leaving the trees closing behind us, until we reached the open field.

"That was amazing," Kenneth said, looking back at the trees. "And they are all back in the same place."

"Kenneth, this is my grandmother Kina, and her friend Nuru," I said.

"Hi, I'm Kenneth," he said.

"Let's get right to business," Nuru said. She pulled out a map. "Here's the exact spot I need you to place the heart." She circled it. "Only you can do this Zuri," she said, eyeing Kenneth.

"Once placed into the earth and covered, you have exactly one minute to get out of there. I'm not sure how the earth may react to it. You guys look out for each other, you hear me. Zuri, do not run super speed unless it's absolutely necessary, do you understand?" Nuru sounded cautious. I nodded my head. "I don't want anyone seeing you do this. Here's money in case you need to buy something. Kenneth, make sure you pack light. Zuri, no extra accessories or anything fancy. Remember, you will be in the 1600s, I don't want you to stick out like a sore thumb, as it may slow you down. Does anyone know how to make a fire?"

"I think I do," Kenneth said. He looked around for something to start a fire.

"I got it," I said, and pushed a tree over before pulling a load of branches over almost instantly, placing them on the ground, and standing the tree back up.

"Are you forgetting something Zuri?" granny asked.

"Oh yea." I turned around back to the tree... thank you," I said as I patted it.

Kenneth stood there with his mouth open. "Wow, strong and fast, can you fly?"

"Nope, I tried," I laughed.

"Yea, that would be really cool if you could fly too, what else can you do?" he asked.

"Well I'm still learning everything, so far I'm fast, strong, and can hear really far, but hopefully soon I ca….," Nuru cleared her throat, cutting me off, "……the fire." she said.

"Right," Kenneth said as he gathered all of the branches and placed them in a pile. He then rubbed them together super-fast, creating friction and causing sparks. He slowed down and blew into the heating wood causing soft puffs of smoke to drift into the air. He slowly placed small dry branches onto the pile and a small flame emerged.

"Good," said Nuru. "In case it gets cold or you need some type of lighting. Kenneth, do your parents know where you are?"

"Ya, they do," he answered.

"You guys need to take this very seriously," Nuru said. "No funny business. No playing around. This is a big responsibility, do you understand?"

"Yes," we said in unison.

"Kenneth, go pack, only bring the items that you need, and be here tomorrow at 8 am sharp. Wear sneakers, bring a hat, the sun may be beaming. I'll see you tomorrow." Nuru dismissed us both and dashed off.

"Is she ok, granny?" I asked.

"Nuru's fine, she's just a little nervous," grandma said.

"Nervous that I won't be safe?" I inquired.

"No, nervous about you taking Kenneth. I assured her you guys will be fine. Kenneth seems like a decent young man. He's kind of cute too," granny said, nudging me and smirking.

"Eeeeeew, granny, Kenneth is my friend," I said.

"Alright, alright," was granny's reply, still smirking.

"You ready?" I asked Kenneth, who was staring at a tree.

"Yea," he said, "I'm ready. How do you move this thing? Its roots are planted pretty firmly; it looks like it took hundreds of years to grow."

"Because I am the tree, Kenneth," I said. We both looked at each other and laughed. I parted the trees, grabbed Kenneth, and dashed toward the house with granny right behind us.

"Would you like to stay for dinner?" I asked.

"I would love to, but seeing that we have to get up so early I should probably head home and get everything together," was his reply.

"Good idea," I said. We hugged and Kenneth jumped on his bike and headed home, all the while being followed by Nuru.

Nuru followed him all the way until he reached his destination—Utabica Air Force Base. She watched as Kenneth got checked by a guard, before entering the gate.

She then dashed back to Kina's home. Kina stood waiting for Nuru in the backyard.

"Did you see anything?" Kina asked.

"No, nothing. He went onto the military base," Nuru said.

"He's probably just a regular ol' boy, Nuru," Kina insisted. "Don't be so uptight."

"You're right Kina, I just don't want anything to go wrong. I wasn't expecting anyone else to go with Zuri. This alone could alter history," Nuru said.

"Zuri is a bright girl, have more faith, she's a Zenzi," Kina assured her.

Chapter 9 🖤

I stood there hand in hand with Nuru and granny. I could tell grandma was nervous.

"I know you will do fine, Zuri. You're smart, trust your heart, trust your judgment, and let it guide you. Now, if you have any trouble or danger I want you to open the portal and come back, ok?" "I won't be disappointed Zuri, your safety is the most important thing to me" she said. "And no matter what, you two stick together. Are you sure you're ok? Do you need another day of training? Do you have everything? Do you need to use the restroom before you go....?" grandma went on and on.

"Granny, granny, granny, I'll be fine," I laughed.

"I have everything," I said as I tightened the straps on my backpack.

Nuru opened the portal and I gave each of them a hug. "I'll be right back," I said.

Kenneth went in before me and held his hand out to help me through. I grabbed his hand and went through the portal. I looked back at them once more waved and blew a kiss at my nervous grandmother. The portal closed.

I pulled out my map to try to see if I could figure out exactly where we were.

"I think we are here," Kenneth said, pointing at one area on the map.

"Ah," I said. I marked the spot. I rolled up my map, placed it into my backpack, and we headed north. My necklace was shining extremely bright red, the brightest I had ever seen it. I tucked it inside my shirt, I didn't need anything bringing me attention or slowing me down.

It looked a lot different, everything looked old. There were none of the huge buildings I was used to seeing, and all the roads seemed to be made of dirt.

"Thanks for bringing me along," said Kenneth. "This is so cool. I'm glad I came to Africa... and maybe you're not so loony after all," he joked. "I didn't believe you until just now. And maybe this is not even real," he said. "Maybe I'm dreaming."

I pinched him.

"Ok, definitely not dreaming," he said. "Can we grab something to eat?" he asked. "I was kind of excited, I forgot to eat."

"Yea, I am a little hungry too," I said. We walked about five miles, saw a nearby diner and stepped inside. The bell rang as we opened the door.

I didn't think diner's existed in the 1600's. I do remember grandma saying Utabica was advanced for its time and a lot of the things we have today originated here.

"Hey, kids," an elderly lady said. We proceeded to the breakfast bar and took a seat.

"It's kind of busy here today," I said.

"Yep, everyone has come from all over to join the festival tonight," the lady said.

"There's a festival tonight?" I asked.

"Yes child, where have you been?" she teased as she placed two napkins in front of us.

"I'll have a water," I said.

"Me too," said Kenneth.

"Alright kids, my name is Naomi and I will be your waitress. Take a look over the menus, I'll be right back with those waters," she said.

"None of this looks appealing to me," I whispered.

"Me either," said Kenneth. "What is a kompoo?"

"I don't know, but I don't want anything that ends with poo," I said, and we both giggled.

Naomi came back with our drinks. "I'll just have a salad," I said as I closed my menu.

"And you, young man?" asked Naomi.

"I'll have the Telu fish with brown rice," said Kenneth.

"Very well then." She took our menus and headed to place our orders.

"What on earth did you just order?" I asked.

"I have no idea," he said. "But fish is fish, right?"

"I sure hope so," I replied.

I heard the bell once more as someone entered the diner.

"Geo!" someone called out in greeting.

"Geo?" I said softly to myself. His name sounded so familiar.

"How are the boys?" I heard somebody ask.

"They are doing well, training is going great," the man said as he took the empty stool beside me.

"I'll have the usual," he said.

"That's Geo," I said to myself. "He tried to get rid of my grandmother."

I stretched out my arms to yawn, and my ice-cold water fell right into Geo's lap.

"OooooWe," he said as he jumped up from his seat.

"I'm so sorry," I said. "I can be so clumsy."

He gave me a stern look.

"Here's your food, kids," Naomi said as she placed our food in front of us. "Enjoy. And I'll bring you another water, sweetie," she added.

"So, the boys and I are going to take another look around the caves for Kina," Geo said as he sipped his tea.

"Still haven't found her yet, huh?" said another waitress.

"Not yet. I have a feeling she'll be around sooner or later," replied Geo.

"And what will you do when you find her?" I asked as Kenneth nudged me.

"Well, Ms. Lady. We are going to have to see why she betrayed our tribe. And take reasonable action from there," Geo said sharply.

"And how do you know she betrayed the tribe?" I asked.

"You haven't been around much, have you?" he asked me. "What's your name?"

"That is none of your concern," I said.

He chuckled. "Well it's no doubt you are a Zenzi. Strong-minded young lady, aren't you?" he said. "Well, when I arrived back to the cave, Kina was missing and the beast was dead. They were in some type of cahoots if you ask me. Something is going on and I will find out," he added.

"Well if you ask me, as long as the beast is gone there is nothing to worry about. Wasn't that the big deal? To get rid of the beast? Kina is a hero. You should just let her be if she's still alive. I think maybe you're afraid she'll come back for you," I said to him. Geo shifted in his seat. "I don't think she's worried about you, Mr. Geo. She's lost her son and her husband. I think you just need something to do to feel important now that the beast is gone, you have nothing," I went on.

Kenneth quickly cut in, "Ooooookay, thanks for the meal, Ms. Naomi. Here's the tab. We'll be on our way, thank you, thank you, excuse me." Kenneth grabbed our bags, grabbed me, and we left the diner.

"Zuri" he exclaimed. "What was that?"

"I'm protecting Kina, he doesn't know a thing," I said.

"Zuri, it's ok," Kenneth said. "Everything will be reset once we get you to the cave. Don't go stirring up anymore unnecessary trouble."

"I guess you're right, Kenneth," I said. "I don't know what's come over me. Let's just get the necklace to the cave. But can we stay for the festival?"

"I don't think there's time," he said.

"It will only set us back about two hours," I said in reply. "Besides, we are like two days ahead. I have a speedy plan to get us there ahead of time."

"Didn't your grandmother say not to use speed unless necessary?" he asked.

"Well it will be necessary if we aren't on time, Kenneth," I said to him. "Come on!" I grabbed his arm as we headed toward the festivities.

"If you say so, Zuri," he said, shaking his head.

We walked down the path, not too far from the diner, and there were several booths set up. One in particular caught my eye. It had a heart necklace. Sort of like mine, but there was no copper around it. I walked over to the table.

"Hello, there," I said to the girl sitting behind the booth. She had to be about my age. "These necklaces are beautiful; did you make them?"

"Yes, I did," she said. "They are to represent hope and peace"

"That's wonderful," I said. "What are you hoping for?"

"I hope that Kina is ok," she replied. "I don't think she betrayed us," the girl whispered. "I think she saved us all."

"I believe the same thing," I told her. "What do the others think of your booth?"

"Well a lot of them are angry about it," she said. "I don't pay that any mind, though. A lot of other girls in my school believe Kina is innocent too."

"How long has it been again?" I asked. "You know, since Kina disappeared?"

"It will be three months now," she said.

"Well I believe Kina is a hero, too," I said. "And don't worry, there will be peace soon."

"I'm Ariel," she said as she extended her hand.

"I'm Zuri, and this is my friend Kenneth," I said.

"Nice to meet you," she replied.

We took a few moments to look at the jewelry then Kenneth and I headed further into the festival, stopping at different booths, playing games and tasting different foods. I even got my face painted like a Zenzi warrior. There was a band playing and Kenneth and I danced, losing track of time, until it fell dark. We saw everyone gathered around in a circle only to find Geo standing in the center addressing the crowd.

"Hundreds of years our tribe has suffered from the big beast. He killed many of our own our fathers, our brothers, our ancestors. The beast is now gone but we will never forget the horror he caused our tribe!" Geo shouted.

As he was speaking, a group of men pushed forward a statue of the beast made of tree branches.

"We will never forget!" he said, as he struck a match and lit the statue. All I could think of was Nuru as the flames engulfed the stick figure I slowly backed away from the crowd.

"Are you ok?" Kenneth asked.

"Let's go, Kenneth," Let's go!"

We pushed through the crowd and hurried out of sight. When we were in the clear, I grabbed Kenneth and zipped far off into the woods. I threw my backpack down.

"It's ok, Zuri, everything will be ok," he said. I paced back and forth.

"These people have no idea," I said. "No idea of the real story. They are being misguided by that Geo!" I said. "I think we are going to call it a night tonight," I said. "It's a little too dark right now to do any traveling."

"Yea, I agree, and all that zipping has made me tired," Kenneth said.

"Oh, please, you didn't do anything but look like this," I said, and made a surprised face with big, wide eyes.

"Ha ha," he said. "That wind slaps you around," he said. "I should have taken some pilot goggles from the Air Force Base."

"How about a snack?" I said.

"Snack? You packed snacks?" was his reply.

"Something like that," I said.

"Didn't they say only pack what you needed?" he teased.

"Well I do need a snack, right about now. Just shut up and make a fire," I said. "I brought s'mores," I chuckled.

"Um, I need branches, Zuri, everybody can't move trees like you," he laughed.

I looked around, took a deep breath, and then jumped really high and grabbed many branches from the tree. It felt as if I moved in slow motion.

"That's new," I said, landing on the ground.

"So you never did that before?" Kenneth asked, as he took the branches and started rubbing them together.

"Nope. I just thought I could do it, and it happened," I said. "Your mind is a powerful thing. I'm not saying to what extent you'll gain powers, but in anything you do Kenneth, you just have to believe it yourself and it will happen."

We sat there and ate our s'mores from the fire, and talked. "Let's get some rest," I said. I dug two hammocks out of my bag and tied them to the trees. I sat in my hammock and continued to talk until I fell asleep.

Kenneth placed my blanket over me, got in his hammock, and covered himself with his own blanket. He sighed. "Goodnight Zuri."

Chapter 10 ♥

Waking up to the sunrise, I looked over to see an empty hammock. I jumped out of my hammock and looked around. Where was Kenneth? I saw that he hadn't taken his things. Maybe someone had gotten him. I looked for my backpack. It was under me.

"Kenneth?" I called.

I looked around, he was nowhere in sight. I looked in my backpack and everything was still there. I was so nervous. I quietly searched the surrounding area to see if I could spot him. I didn't see him anywhere. I tuned everything out and I could hear footsteps coming toward me. I jumped up on a high thick branch and waited for what was to come.......

"Hello? Anybody there?" I recognized that voice. It was Kenneth. I jumped down out of the tree.

"Kenneth!" I said. He jumped.

"Don't you ever scare me like that!" he said.

"Where did you go, why didn't you wake me?" I asked him.

"I only stepped away for a second," he said. "I went to go fill up our water bottles – see?" he said, holding them up. "I didn't want to wake you for something silly," he said. "I was going to wake you when I came back."

"Just don't do that again ok?" I said in reply. "What if someone had captured you on your way there? Or snuck up on me while I was asleep? We have to stick together at all times. All times...no exceptions, ok?"

"I'm sorry, Zuri, I didn't think of it that way," he said.

We packed away our blankets and hammocks. I located on the map exactly where we were, and we headed in that direction.

"You never really talked about your family. How's your mom? Do you have any siblings?" I asked him as we walked.

"Well, I don't have any siblings," he said. "I mean its cool most of the time. My mom, she's still back in D.C. She has to work; I think she will be able to make it here one of these weekends. I always feel like my parents don't understand me. My dad is so wrapped up in the military he barely has time to talk about anything else or the things that I'm interested in. He wants me to be in the military when I get out of high school and get my education there."

"Well, what do you want to do Kenneth?" I asked him.

"You know, Zuri, I'm not sure," came his reply. "No one has ever asked me that before."

"Well it's a good idea to think about it," I said to him. "You can be whatever you want. Don't let anyone force you to be something, only you know what's best for yourself and what will make you happy."

"Um, Zuri? Are you sure you're not an old lady, are you sure you are only 13 and wasn't brought back?" he teased.

"I'm pretty sure," I said.

We stopped to grab a bite to eat, then got back on track.

"Why couldn't the portal just be opened where the cave was?" asked Kenneth.

"Well, granny wasn't sure exactly where that was. It's been hundreds of years since she's even been back here, it's probably all caved in by now. Or something was probably built in its place. It may have been too risky to open it anywhere else besides granny's backyard," I told him.

"What will you do with your powers once you get back?" he asked.

"Probably join the track team," I joked. "I'm not sure. Hopefully they'll become useful somehow, so that I can help people. Maybe I can cure some sicknesses or something, I always wanted to be a vet. May I can talk to animals or something," I joked.

"You can't tell anyone about your abilities, though. It will bring so much attention, maybe the wrong attention," Kenneth said. "After all, you want to enjoy your childhood now, right?"

"Yea," I said.

"So will you grow old?" was his next question.

"Yea, I will grow old, just after a certain point I don't think I will age unless I choose too. I don't want to live for hundreds of years like granny. I think it will be painful to watch people come and go out of my life. It had to be sad for poor Nuru, she was just a baby and had to grow up alone. I couldn't imagine. I think I would want to go out with my generation now, so I won't have to meet new people every hundred years. Ah, I don't want to talk about death," I said. "It's a scary thing. Especially knowing when it's going to happen."

You're a very smart girl, Zuri," he told me.

I peeped down at my map. We were getting very near the cave. I could feel it, and my necklace lit up through my shirt.

"We're almost there!" I said.

As we got closer to the cave I saw something coming toward us in the distance. I put my arm in front of Kenneth to stop him. The figure grew larger as it came closer. It looked like a lion. But a tad bigger. It came face to face with us and stopped dead in its tracks.

"Zuri, what's going on?" Kenneth said.

"Shhh," I said. The creature and I stared at each other.

"He doesn't trust us," I said. "He thinks we are up to no good."

I stared at the creature and we had a dialogue through our minds without speaking.

"I am Zuri, granddaughter of Kina, a friend of Nuru. I am here to place Nuru's heart into the ground," I said, holding my necklace for the creature to see it.

"Who's the boy?" it asked me.

"He is a friend, he's come to accompany me to make sure I make it safe," I said.

"You cannot trust the boy," the creature replied.

"He's a good friend," I said in protest.

"His heart is not pure, he is dishonest. Turn back, come without him," the creature ordered.

"I can't come without him, we're almost there," I said. "I trust him; he wouldn't harm me. I need to put this into the earth now, I have no other chance. And time is running out."

The creature stared at Kenneth.

"Please, we've come very far, traveled through time and we are so close to completing this task," I urged the creature.

"What's it saying, Zuri?" Kenneth asked.

"He doesn't trust you, says you are being dishonest," I told him.

"What does he mean dishonest? About what?" asked Kenneth.

"He told me to come back without you," I said.

"But I didn't ask to come, you asked me to come," he replied.

"I know," I said. "Maybe I can get him to budge." I began to speak back to the creature.

"Since you cannot trust him, can you come with us, and make sure everything is ok? You can keep an eye on him. Who are you anyway?" I asked.

"I am Nile, guard of Nuru's cave. I cannot enter the cave, I can only stand guard outside to protect it from tribes who may try to destroy it. Only you may enter. The boy must stay."

"But Nile!" I said aloud.

"What's he saying now, Zuri?" asked Kenneth.

"Kenneth, I think it would be best if you stayed right here. I don't want to cause any trouble," I told him.

"Didn't you just say stick together at all times?" he said in reply.

"I'll go ahead, and I promise I'll zip back after it's completed," I told him.

"I can't allow you to go up there alone, Zuri! We have to stick together, remember?! I'm not leaving you," he said.

"I can handle it, Kenneth," I told him.

"I don't think so," was his reply. "Tell him; tell him that I mean no harm. Tell him I'll keep you safe."

As I was about to relay the message I saw the creature growl and jump at Kenneth, who by now was holding a knife.

"NO, KENNETH! PUT IT DOWN! STOP IT!" I yelled.

I heard scuffling and growling as he wrestled the lion.

"NO!" I shouted.

I had to do something. I looked around but there was really nothing I could grab. We were out in an open space. I watched as Nile swiped Kenneth with his large paw. In response, Kenneth swung his knife cutting Nile on his side before he fell to the ground. Both Kenneth and Nile were badly injured. Nile gathered himself and began charging once more towards Kenneth.

Desperate, I took my hands and hit the ground. This caused the ground to rumble and split open. The lion-like creature fell to the ground on its side. Both Kenneth and the lion were now lain on the ground. I rushed to Kenneth's side to check his pulse. He was not breathing.

"No, no, no, no, come on Kenneth, breathe," I urged him. "Come on, come on!"

I pushed on his chest and put my head to his heart. "Come onnnnn, come onnnn!" I shouted.

I proceeded to do CPR. It was hopeless. I began to cry.

"Kenneth!" I sobbed. I sat beside him with my head in my hands, crying hysterically. I turned back over to him. "Come on," I pleaded. I grabbed his limp hand but it simply fell back down.

"No, no, no, this can't be!" I shouted.

I checked for his pulse, nothing. I rubbed my necklace, closed my eyes, and placed both hands onto Kenneth's heart. I swayed back and forth, breathing deeply and slowly, in and out. I took very deep breaths, still holding his heart. Deep breaths. I began to feel dizzy but I stayed focused. Just then, I felt him move. My eyes shot open, and Kenneth was looking up at me.

"Z, Z, Z, Zuri?" he asked.

"Kenneth! Oh my goodness! You're alive! Kenneth!" I yelled as I handed him a water. I dug in my bag and grabbed my first aid kit to bandage his injuries.

"You scared me so much, oh my goodness!" I said. I squeezed him tight.

"Ow, ow, ow," he said.

"Sorry," I laughed with glee.

"Zuri? Did I just-? Did you just-? Zuri, you brought me back?" he asked, puzzled.

"Yes," I said, shaking my head and wiping my tears. "Are u ok?"

"I'm fine, are u ok?" he asked.

"I feel a little weak," I said.

"Sit down, Zuri," he said as he got up.

"No, I don't have time, Kenneth, I have to finish. I have to finish this," I told him.

As I tried to get up, I looked over at the lion and saw that it was still breathing, but not very well. As I walked toward the lion, Kenneth grabbed me.

"Zuri?"

"Yes," I said.

"Thank you," he said.

"You're welcome," I replied.

I walked over to the almost-lifeless creature, and placed my hands on it.

"Zuri, don't," Kenneth said.

"I have to," I said. "I feel in my heart that I need to help him, Kenneth. He was here for a purpose."

I placed my hands over the lion's body and concentrated. I focused hard, and then it all went black.

Chapter 11 ♥

I opened my eyes and I was in an unfamiliar place. I had a cool rag on my head. I jumped up, trying to figure out where I was. I was in a room. I sat up from the bed and looked around. Where was my backpack? Where was Kenneth? Where was Nile the lion creature? Where was I? The room was very plain, all it had was a bed, a desk, and a chair and red flower wallpaper. I heard a familiar voice and I followed it carefully and quietly. I heard it coming from down a hall. I moved quickly but very quietly until I reached the end of the hall.

"But she literally saved my life!" I heard.

"I don't care," someone shot back. "We now have what we were after," the voice said.

"I'm not helping you anymore, mom! This is not right."

"Give me the necklace," the voice said.

I reached for my necklace and noticed that it had gone. I turned the corner to see Ms. Zuba and Kenneth struggling for the necklace.

"Kenneth? Ms. Zuba?" I asked.

"Well hello, Ms. Zuri," she said with a smile, swinging my necklace back and forth in her hand. I made a grab for it and she yanked it back.

"What's going on here, Kenneth?" I asked. "Is that your mom?"

"Zuri, I can explain," he said. "At first I was trying to help my mother. But then we became really great friends, and now I'm no longer a part of this. I'm so sorry," he said.

"Kenneth, I trusted you," I said. "How could you do this?"

"Should have been a little smarter, missy," Ms. Zuba said. "Besides, Zuri, I'm doing you a favor by taking this off of your hands, possibly saving your life."

"How could you ever save my life?" I asked.

"Zuri, Zuri, Zuri, to be such an intelligent young girl, yet you're so foolish. You see, your job is to put this here necklace into the earth so that everything can go back to normal and be as it was supposed to be, right?" asked Ms. Zuba.

I looked at Kenneth, who was looking down at his feet. How could he tell her everything! It was a secret.

"Right," she answered for me. "Right, now, if everything is how it's supposed to be Zuri, you would not even have been born. You see, if you put the necklace in the earth the beast dies, your grandmother dies, and, guess what, if your grandmother dies, she can't bring your dad back to life, meaning you or

116

your little brother wouldn't have been born," she laughed. "So I'll just take this out of your hands, put it in the ground, and you and your granny, your brother, and your dad all live." She smiled an evil grin. "Easy, right?"

"See, Zuri," Kenneth began. "I didn't want to be a part of this, but my mother told me that if you do this you may die and I didn't want that to happen," he pleaded. "I promise, after a while I was going to just go with you and not even meet up with her. I brought you here because I didn't know where else to take you. You were unconscious, I didn't know anyone else who could help."

"Give me my necklace back," I demanded.

"No," said Ms. Zuba. "Shall I help you return through the portal?" she asked.

"I'm not going anywhere without my necklace," I told her. "Now, we can do this the easy way, or we can do it the hard way," I said.

"Hmm, although both ways sound tempting, Zuri, I'll choose to do it my way," she said.

Ms. Zuba stepped toward the door, and I followed her, but then stopped. Something was holding me back. It felt as if some sort of force field was preventing me from moving forward. "What is this?" I asked as I tried to pass the threshold. I hit my hands against the invisible wall.

Ms. Zuba laughed. "Have fun, Zuri," she said as she waved. "I'll take good care of your necklace, and I'll take care of you later," she said to Kenneth as she disappeared out of the door.

"Ah!" I ran back, and then charged, but got pushed right back to the same place I had come from. I couldn't follow her, I tried and tried .... And tried and tried. And I could not get out.

"Zuri," Kenneth said. "It's no hope."

I turned around and glared at him. "There is hope," I said. "There is a way I can get through this."

"It wears off in about four hours," he said with his head hung.

I went around to the windows to try to escape but the force field was blocking the whole house. I sat down on the floor with my head in my hands. I felt disappointed in myself, I knew I had to get out of there. I didn't want to let my grandmother or Nuru down. Though what Ms. Zuba had said did seem very true. If things did go back to normal, how could my dad exist? How could I exist if he didn't?

I looked up to see that Kenneth was trying to get out of the force field and that he was stuck behind it as well.

"I'm very sorry, Zuri, really, really sorry. I thought I was saving your life. Do you forgive me? I can help you. We can get through this together," he pleaded with me.

"I don't trust you and I don't want or need your help. I don't know why I ever trusted you! I begged and tried to convince them to let you come with me. That was a huge mistake!" I said as I sat on the floor with my head in my hands.

"Zuri?" asked Kenneth.

"Don't talk to me, Kenneth, we're no longer friends. Come to think about it, we were never friends, you just used me to get information out of me. This whole friendship was just a big lie. I don't believe anything you ever said to me," I told him.

"I needed information at first, Zuri. I was trying to help my mom. But I started making my own decisions. I promise, I stopped being on board with her a long time ago," he tried to explain.

"I don't want to hear anything else you have to say," I said. "It's probably a lie anyway."

"If I were lying Zuri, and I was still a part of this, why would she lock her own son behind this force field?!" he asked.

"I wouldn't doubt that you can really get out of here. You probably know spells too!" I shot back at him.

Kenneth looked down. "Well I do know a few spells that my mom taught me. But I never use them. And she only taught me what she wanted me to know. I won't be able to get out for four hours, Zuri, just like you. See?" He charged toward the door several times, and was knocked back down each time. "See?" he asked.

"Well, I won't be here for four hours with you Kenneth," I said, and grabbed my backpack. "I have something to do."

I was a Zenzi, I could not give up. I had a purpose. As I sat there with my eyes closed I listened to the trees whistling. I connected with them. I became it. I could feel the breeze on my skin and threw my hair. I felt free and danced in the breeze. I meditated and became one with the tree. I could feel the breeze, but this time it was more natural; I could smell the air, my hair blew. ...wait a minute, my hair blew!

I opened my eyes and there I was; outside, in a tree. It was a little weird but cool at the same time. I threw my backpack to the ground, then jumped down after it. I looked around. It looked as if I was right outside of Ms. Zuba's house. I thanked the tree. Then laughed at myself, did I really just thank a tree? I don't think I'll ever get used to this.

I don't know how I got to Ms. Zuba's house, or whatever house I was in, so I didn't know which way to go. Toward the beast cave? I had no idea where I was. Seemed as if I was at square one, and time was surely running out. "I can do this," I said. I stood there a while, zoning out, meditating, thinking, and trusting nature and trusting my heart and trusting that they would guide me in the right direction.

"LET'S GO," I said, as I zipped through the wind.

Meanwhile, Ms. Zuba was truly pleased with herself. She felt excited to finally have her hands on the necklace and dreamed about how she might be able to change history and have the powers of the great beast. Her tribe would have the strongest woman. Her future granddaughters would surely have her power. She would choose to live forever!

As she drove towards the cave, her tire suddenly popped and flattened.

"No, No, No, no, not right now!" she shouted.

She pulled over to the side of the road to see that three of her tires were completely flat. Really, of all the times to get a flat, I get not one but three right now!" she said. She got out of the car and began to walk a little. "Car trouble wouldn't stop me" she said.

She grew very weary and thirsty. "What should I do with my new powers." She thought aloud. "Maybe I'd rule the world."

After what seemed like several hours she reached in her bag and got out the map she took from Zuri. "Hmmm, doesn't seem too far from here." She rolled it back up and put it into her bag.

As she made her long journey to the cave, a creature in the distance headed towards her. 'It kind of looks like a lion' she thought. 'Only bigger.'

"Get out of my way," she told it. "Move along! Shoo!" she shouted. "I have some business to take care of."

It growled as it came toward her. "You think I came this long way to get frightened by some animal. I don't think so," she said to the mysterious creature.

She did a force field spell and stopped the creature dead in its tracks. "This is far too easy," she said as she walked right past it. It roared and growled but couldn't quite reach her. "Ha!" she laughed.

'This whole trip is literally taking candy from babies.' she thought. She began to think about her son Kenneth and how she would deal with him later. He was never as strong as her. She knew he'd probably get soft and try to bail out on the plan, which is the reason she had a plan B. The force field spell. 'Oh well, he and his little friend would both thank me later.'

It was time to put her plan into action. She was tired but felt as if victory would be hers. Ms. Zuba walked towards the cave with a huge grin on her face. But the cave wasn't there. She was sure this is what it had said on the map. She looked back down to confirm that this was indeed the place.

"You finally arrived," she heard a voice say.

Chapter 12 🖤

"Zuri! What a pleasant surprise!" said Ms. Zuba.

"Is it?" I said as I stood up to see her sitting on the rock. "What took you so long Zuba, if that is your real name?" I asked.

"So you made it out of the force field?" she said. "Impressive. Girl's got skills. Too bad they will be wasted," she said. "And too bad you're going to be destroyed now. See Zuri, once again I tried to protect you but I see you just don't appreciate my kindness. You could have just stayed there and when the time expired jumped back into your little portal and gone home. But no, you just want to be a stubborn little Zenzian, huh?" she laughed. "Well I'll have no mercy on you."

"And what exactly would I need your mercy for?" I asked. "Just give me my necklace Zuba, and I promise I won't destroy you. It's not too late," I said.

"So sorry, Zuri. I'm afraid I can't do that, you see. You wouldn't harm a fly anyway. The power will now be mine," she replied.

"Let's see about that," I said as I hit the ground, and Zuba fell to her feet. She immediately jumped back up. This caused dust to come up from the ground and reveal the invisible cave. Zuba spotted it and began running towards it. I chased her with my lightning speed cutting her off and blocking her from coming near the cave's entrance. She kept trying to move past me but I kept zipping in front of her blocking her from the entry to the cave.

"Move, Zuri!" she shouted.

"Ms. Zuba, I really don't want to hurt you. Just give me the necklace. You don't even know if it will work. You see, only a Zenzi can put it into the ground. That's the way it's supposed to be. If you put it there it may react badly. Just give me the necklace. We can both be safe," I said.

"No!" she yelled, and ran toward the cave, and I kept zipping around her and stopping her in her tracks. "You've been warned, Zuri!" She threw a punch as I ducked and clipped her with my foot. I tried to pull the necklace off of her neck but it wouldn't break!

She pulled me to the ground and as we tumbled back and forth she broke free, jumped up, and ran inside the cave. Once again I zipped past her and stopped her in her tracks. "Give me my necklace!" I shouted. This time I was able to snatch it from her neck and used my lightning speed to zip around her and deeper into the cave. I had a few minutes before she caught up to me.

I couldn't pinpoint the exact location of where to bury the necklace and the last of Nuru's heart. I patted and searched the ground nervously in the darkness of the cave. I began to panic as Ms. Zuba's footsteps came closer. Suddenly the necklace began to glow. I had to be at the right spot. Having no time to get materials out of my backpack I kneeled to the ground and feverishly began to dig with my hand. I gently placed the necklace into the earth, and covered it with the copper-colored dust.

"Noooooo," I heard Zuba scream from behind me.

The cave began to shake. I turned to face Ms. Zuba.

"Come on, get out of here!" I told her.

She pushed passed me.

"Come on!" I said again trying to grab her. She ran around me, and as the cave began to shake, she dropped to her knees and attempted to dig for the necklace.

"Stop!" I said. "Stop it!"

The cave shook violently and I knew I had to escape. I glanced at Zuba one last time and zipped out of the cave just as ceiling and walls began to crumble. I watched in awe as the cave collapsed in a huge cloud of dust and dirt.

Granny told me to leave as soon as it was done, but what if Zuba was able to reach the necklace? What if she was able to dig it out? I just had to find out!

Suddenly a huge beast-like creature came out of the cave. It was fuzzy and gray with four huge paws! The beast was holding the necklace!

"See what you've done, little girlllll?!" it growled. "Look at me! This was not supposed to happen! You have ruined everything!"

You should have left the necklace where it was," I shouted angrily.

The beast hit the ground, shaking the earth and causing me to fall. She ran toward me at lightning speed. I channeled my gymnastic lessons and somersaulted out of her reach! I leaped onto her back, using all of my strength to knock her over. But she was too strong...she recovered quickly and swatted me away like a fly. The force of her smack knocked me two miles away before I came crashing to the ground. She charged towards me on all four of her legs. I quickly pull a huge tree from its roots and hit her like a baseball. She was so stunned upon impact that she released the necklace. I jumped to catch the necklace in midair.

"Got it!" I exclaimed

"Give me that necklace, Zuri!" she shouted.

I had to find a way to get the necklace back where it belonged, the cave.

I zipped back toward the cave with Zuba hot on my trail. Just as I reached what used to be the cave entrance I made a sharp turn, causing Zuba to run head first into a wall of rubble.

"It's all over, Zuba!" I shouted.

As Zuba charged for me, I quickly grabbed my knife out of my side pocket and wrestled the beast. I managed to knock her on her back and swiftly stabbed the beast in its heart.

126

She let out a horrific howl and knocked me off of her, flinging me miles across open field and plains.

I landed against a huge, hard stone.

Everything was very faint. I couldn't hear anything. My vision was foggy and my blinks were long, but I could see the beast heading towards me in what seemed like slow motion.

I looked in my hands to see that I still had the necklace. Maybe I should just throw it to buy me some time. I knew I would heal shortly, but I was already too weak. What would I be buying time for? I needed to take care of everything right away, but I didn't know how my healing process would be. But what could I do, once she reached me? I didn't feel like I could move.

I could hear a voice inside of me encouraging me not to give up. 'I can't let granny down' I thought, and 'What about Nuru?' I tried to get up but the pain was so bad. I hadn't quite gotten all of my energy back since I had brought Kenneth back to life. Maybe it would take longer for me to heal this time.

"This can't be it," I said to myself. My eyelids were so heavy. "This can't be."

The beast was getting closer and closer until I saw a figure jump on top of it and wrestle it to the ground. They scuffled around and around. I could tell from its figure it was a man. He was very fast and swift. I used all of my strength and managed to get on my hands and knees. I crawled lazily toward the action.

"Kenneth? Is that you?" I asked.

"No, I'm right here, Zuri," he said, running from behind me. He put his arm around my shoulder, and helped me get up. I leaned on him for balance. "Are you ok?" he asked with a very worried look.

"How did you get here?" I asked.

"Don't worry, I'll tell u later. Are you ok?" he asked me again.

"Kenneth, if you are here, then who is that? Who did you bring with you?" I said, pointing to the man. I couldn't tell who it was through all the dust. I took a deep breath, blew into the air, and as the dust cleared I could see it was my dad! Oh no! I felt as if I had my second wind, stood up straight, and zipped toward the beast to help my dad.

"Catch, Zuri!" Kenneth shouted, throwing me a thick chain. "Wrap its legs!"

I zipped, weaving in and out of the beast's legs until I was back on my father's side.

"PULL!" I shouted. My dad and I both pulled the chain as the beast tried to break through. It growled. My dad and I pulled with all of our might. "Ahhhhh," we groaned. The chain suddenly felt easier to pull. I turned to see that Kenneth was now helping us.

"Come on guys, pull. Pull harder!" Kenneth said. All the while the beast was still struggling to break free. "Ahhhh!" we all shouted. Again the chain got lighter, a lot lighter, until we were able to knock the beast down. My dad rushed and climbed on top of the tangled beast and drove his knife into its heart. As he did this the beast let out a howl, which caused my dad to fly off, and I rushed to catch him.

"Dad! Are you ok?" I asked. He opened his eyes.

"Yes, I'm fine," he said.

"You did a good job, warrior," I heard a man say.

As he dropped the chain from his hands, I looked up to see Geo.

"Geo!? What are you doing here?" I asked.

"Well, your friend came and got me, said he needed my help. He told me that you were in trouble. He told me that he was from the future and what you were trying to do. Of course, I didn't believe him and sent him away, that's until he came back with Abdul. Who just happened to be an 18-year-old boy who passed away three months ago, but now he is about my age. In fact, I thought that this was some kind of joke, but Abdul remembered things only my tribe could have taught him. He told me his daughter was in trouble. I decided if I didn't help I would be going against the very things that I taught, that we are family and we must stick together. Besides, Abdul saved my life! So shortly he and your friend left, I rushed to get here to help." Geo explained.

"Thanks Geo," I said, hugging him.

I looked up to see Kenneth staring at the slain beast. I didn't take into consideration that he had just lost his mom. He went over to it and touched it. He sat beside it, placed his head in his hands, and began to sob. I went over to him and touched his shoulder.

"I'm so sorry, Kenneth," I said. I sat beside him to offer comfort.

"I just felt like it was the right thing to do" he said with his head in his hands.

My dad came over and touch Kenneth's shoulder.

"I'm truly sorry for your loss Kenneth. It took a lot of heart to do what you have done and I truly appreciate it. You will always have my respect young man. If you need anything, anything at all. We will always be here for you" my dad said to him.

"Yes, thanks Kenneth, I really appreciate it. I know it wasn't easy." I added. I also want to thank you for getting Geo and my dad.

"Well I found a spell book lying around while I was stuck in the house for the four hours. Nothing on getting out of force fields, ironically, but I can tell you everything you need to know about a portal," he said. "Besides, we stick together at all times, no exceptions."

I knew that must have been difficult to do, I wished I knew exactly what to say. But I didn't know what I could say to make things any better.

"I'll be right back," I said.

I grasped the necklace in my hands and went over to the location of the cave. I dug once more, deeper this time, and placed the necklace into the ground. "Now that Nuru's heart is in the ground, she can be at peace with her family," I said as I buried it.

"You guys ready? Let's go!" I said. I opened the portal and walked toward it. "Come on, Kenneth," I said, turning back to him. He looked at the beast and looked back at me.

"I think I'm going to stay here, Z," he said.

"You can't stay here Kenneth! You don't belong now, stop playing and let's go," I said.

"No. I'm staying," he replied.

"Kenneth, you have to come back, you don't know anyone here!" I shouted to him.

"I don't have anything or anyone to go back home to," he replied. "My dad barely spends any time with me, or pays me any attention. At least here I can start over." he said.

"I'll take care of him," Geo said, resting his hand on his shoulder.

"Just go, Zuri. I want to stay here," Kenneth said, as he rested his hand on the beast.

I walked over to him, and gave him a long hug. "Are you sure?" I asked.

"Yes, I'm sure. See you later," he said.

"See you later? I sure hope so," I said.

My dad shook hands with Geo "Thanks" he said.

"No problem warrior" Geo responded.

"Please don't tell anyone what happened." I said to Geo and Kenneth.

"We won't." Geo said.

My dad and I held hands as we entered the portal, I waved to Kenneth until it was completely shut.

Chapter 13 ♥

On our walk home through the long tree pathway, my dad and I talked.

"So did you know you were Abdul from the storybooks the whole time?" I asked him.

"Not exactly," he said. "All your friend had to do was come to me and tell me that you were in trouble. I dropped everything and followed him. Something just clicked, you know?"

"Yea," I said.

"You did a good job, young warrior princess," he said. "I'm so proud of you. Who trained you, your granny?" he laughed as he kissed me on the forehead.

"Yes, she trained me. She's pretty cool, for an old lady," I laughed. "Did you know about Nuru? Do you remember being a kid?"

"I used to have flashbacks, well, dreams, as a teen," he said. "That I was some type of fighter. But I figured they were just dreams. I've heard the story of the big beast, but never really paid attention, ya know? I'm very proud of you, Zuri. You are beautiful, intelligent, courageous, and driven. It takes a lot of guts to do what you did. You know you and your little brother would be a great power team? If you two got together – brains and power. The world had better watch out!"

"That's if we can get along for two seconds," I said, and we both laughed.

We arrived at my grandmother's house, and my dad opened the door for me. My mom rushed to me.

"Zuri, are you ok?" she said, feeling my head and my neck and grabbing my hands. "Are you ok, sweetie?" she said as she hugged me.

"Yes mom, I'm fine, why, what's wrong?" I asked.

"Well your grandmother told me you were upset over Ms. Shalo's passing, and you needed some fresh air. And your friend Kenneth came here looking worried and afraid, so your dad went out to look for you. I hadn't realized how close you'd gotten with her," mom said.

"Yes, I'm ok now, mom," I smiled, playing along. "She's at peace."

My mom hugged me as I hugged her back. I could see my grandmother looking at me with a tear in her eye. She quickly wiped it away. My grandmother was a sweetie but a tough cookie.

"You ok, granny?" I asked as I walked toward her.

"I'm doing great," she said, and we hugged. "Zuri, do you have a moment?" she asked as she led me toward the door.

"Sure granny," I said.

We sat outside and my grandmother gave me a huge hug. "You did it Zuri! I'm so proud of you," she said, grabbing my face.

"Thanks grandma, but it didn't go as smoothly as it should have. What if you'd really sent me alone? I wouldn't have been able to do it. I feel like I've failed somehow," I said.

"It's alright, don't beat yourself up about it, everyone needs a little help sometimes. You only fail if you don't try. Don't put it in the atmosphere that you've failed. Look on the bright side of things, Zuri, and don't be too prideful. The fact is that you completed it. Nuru is happy. She lived a long life, and now she is at peace and with her family. Oh, I wish you could have seen it. It was beautiful. A burst of light, it was wonderful. You've done a great thing. Oh, and before I forget, she says thank you and she wanted me to give you this."

My grandmother reached in her pocket and pulled out a beautiful old-fashioned skeleton key. "It's pretty," I said. "What does it do?"

"I don't know, Zuri," she said. "Like everything on earth, it has a purpose and you will know its purpose when the time is right." My grandmother hugged me again.

"I'm getting old, too, Zuri," she went on. "I may want to start my life now. My real life. My ability to grow old. With my family. You know, it's a beautiful thing. I have everything I ever wanted in more than one lifetime. You, your brother, your dad, and your mom have brought me great joy. I don't regret one bit of reserving that heart. That was the best thing that could have happened. I got my life back, I got my son back, and I have you."

My grandmother placed one hand in my hand, and the other on my heart. "I love you Zuri," she said.

My brother was shaking me to get off of the plane. I woke up feeling confused. How did I get here?

"Come on, Zuri. We're back home," Anthony said.

"Where's grandma?" I asked.

"Right here, sweetie, come on," she said as she helped me out of the seat. I was so confused. I didn't know what had happened. If I was dreaming I was so lost. Where was I? Was I coming to Utabica, was I leaving Utabica? Had it all been a dream?

"Come on, Zuri," Anthony said, as he grabbed my arm walking through the airport. "You're walking like a zombie, just like you were at Utabica airport," he said. "It's as if the light's on but nobody's home," my brother said.

"So, are we in D.C. now?" I asked.

"I don't believe this," he said. "How are you the oldest child? Yes – we – are – in – Washing–ton D.C.," he said slowly. I smiled at him and gave him a kiss on his cheek.

"Ewww," he wiped it off -but smiled as I walked away. I dug in my pocket and saw I had the key that my grandmother gave me. I didn't remember getting on the plane. I shook it off, but for some odd reason I felt different – strong and recharged.

When we got back to our house, I was so happy to be home. I ran upstairs, lay in my bed, and took a deep breath. "That was such an adventure," I said, fumbling with the key in my hands. "Looks like another adventure for dun, dun, dundunnnnn, Zuri Nia!" I laughed. "Maybe," I said to myself.

Now back to my normal routine. Well, almost normal. The fact that I'm going to be in high school in a few weeks, that I've managed to have some type of powers, and possibly changed history, and that I went back in time were definitely not normal. As I took a deep breath my mom came up to my room with a package.

"Here, Z," she said. "Guess we got this while we were away. It looks pretty old and damaged, be careful." She placed the small package on my desk.

I looked at the box, it did look very old. It was dusty and in a bad state. A label on it read "To Ms. Beautiful Purpose." I opened the box, which had another smaller box in it, with another smaller box in it, with another smaller box in it, and, finally, a pink mesh bag. It was my necklace! I was so happy to see it, I immediately put it on. I saw a piece of yellow paper in the bag. I opened it and read what it said.

Zuri,

I hoped this worked. The lady at the post office looked at me weird when I said I didn't want this package sent out until 400 years later. Lol. She didn't think that that was even possible. I hope you get it. If not, I'm sure it will find you somehow. Thanks for everything, and sorry again for lying to you. I just wanted to keep you safe. I'm doing fine. Geo is a great guy. I think I was born in the wrong generation, anyway, Utabica in the 1600s is so awesome! I didn't know they had postal service back then. Apparently they are way ahead of time. I know how much you liked your necklace, so I got Ariel to make you one as close to the real one as possible. You know Ariel? The girl who was selling replicas at the festival. I know it will never replace the original one but at least you'll have a reminder. If you ever figure out how to come back, you should come visit sometime. Not sure if it will mess anything up if I come back there. I'll figure it out lol.

Kenneth

P.s. I forgot to tell you how I got out of the force field. No, I didn't lie again, I promise. I was really stuck! Let's just say a wise young lady told me in anything you do, you just have to believe it yourself and it will happen.

I smiled as I closed the letter, and when I looked up, Robyn was standing at my door.

"What's with the goofy grin Robyynnnn!" I said.

"Zuriiiii!" We screamed and hugged each other.

"I missed you sooo much," I said, and we jumped around in a circle.

Anthony passed by the door. "Oh, please," he said, shaking his head.

"So you got to tell me all about your vacay," Robyn said, "but firsssst I have to show you something." She closed my door and hung up a garment bag on the hook on the back of my door. She opened the bag and there was a black sleek-looking outfit with shoulder pads that looked like leaves, brown gloves, a tan wrap skirt, tights, and boots.

"That's nice, Robyn, did you make it for a play or something?" I asked.

"Zuri," she laughed, "I made it for you!"

"ME?!" I said.

"Of course," she replied as she touched the fabric. "Every superhero needs a costume."

"Robyn, I'm no superhero," I told her.

"Are you kidding me?" she said. "You are ZURI NIA, THE Zuri Nia! Super strength, super speed, combat, shall I go on?" she exclaimed.

"Well thanks for thinking of me while I was away," I said, "I'll keep this close."

"But Zuri, you haven't even let me give you the perks," she said.

"Robyn that's a silly-looking outfit," I laughed.

"I think it's cute! This baby won me first place at the portfolio piece we had. It's shock resistant, a wind breaker, fireproof and it dries quickly in case you get in water! It also adapts to all temperatures! This baby won me first place!" she said, patting the outfit. "They tried to pay me to keep it there as an example for future students. But noooo amount of money could have kept it there, I made it specifically for my bestie," she said. "But its ok, I guess I should have taken the offer," she pouted, and held the outfit on its hanger in the air. She gave it one more glance before sighing and reaching for the garment bag to put it away.

"Ok, let me see what you have," I said.

"YAY!" said Robyn. "First, try it on!" I looked at her. "Pleeeeeease," she begged.

"Ok, ok," I replied. "I'll try it on…"

Zuri Nia

...to be continued

Made in the USA
Lexington, KY
13 April 2016